They were pinned

The dogs and trackers came behind them. Men on horseback soon followed. Bolan watched them from behind cover. He clicked his radio. "Piet, what have you got up front?"

"Armed men, platoon strength," Piet said.

Bolan glanced at Gilad. "Anything?"

Gilad and the guide spoke in whispered Russian. Gilad shook his head. "He says he doesn't know who these guys are. He says despite their clothes they are not Tajik."

Bolan surveyed their trackers. "Piet, how are the guys ahead of us armed?"

"It's all Russian kit."

"My guys are all carrying Chinese weapons," Bolan said and clicked his radio. "Eckhart, you there?"

"I copy, Coop."

"I think the people in front and behind are two different groups."

Eckhart wasn't panicking yet but he was clearly agitated. "What are you saying, Coop?"

"I've got a theory these guys h___ ___ ___nt agendas." B___ ___ looked at the ex-Ra___ ___ nd watch what ___

MACK BOLAN ®
The Executioner

The Executioner

Don Pendleton's ®

LETHAL COMPOUND

A GOLD EAGLE BOOK FROM

W☺RLDWIDE®

TORONTO • NEW YORK • LONDON
AMSTERDAM • PARIS • SYDNEY • HAMBURG
STOCKHOLM • ATHENS • TOKYO • MILAN
MADRID • WARSAW • BUDAPEST • AUCKLAND

Recycling programs for this product may not exist in your area.

First edition November 2009

ISBN-13: 978-0-373-64372-1

Special thanks and acknowledgment to Charles Rogers for his contribution to this work.

LETHAL COMPOUND

He who seizes on the moment, he is the right man.
—Johann Goethe
1749–1832
Faust

When the enemy attacks, my only option is to seize whatever opportunity comes my way.
—Mack Bolan

THE
MACK BOLAN

LEGEND

Nothing less than a war could have fashioned the destiny of the man called Mack Bolan. Bolan earned the Executioner title in the jungle hell of Vietnam.

But this soldier also wore another name—Sergeant Mercy. He was so tagged because of the compassion he showed to wounded comrades-in-arms and Vietnamese civilians.

Mack Bolan's second tour of duty ended prematurely when he was given emergency leave to return home and bury his family, victims of the Mob. Then he declared a one-man war against the Mafia.

He confronted the Families head-on from coast to coast, and soon a hope of victory began to appear. But Bolan had broken society's every rule. That same society started gunning for this elusive warrior—to no avail.

So Bolan was offered amnesty to work within the system against terrorism. This time, as an employee of Uncle Sam, Bolan became Colonel John Phoenix. With a command center at Stony Man Farm in Virginia, he and his new allies—Able Team and Phoenix Force—waged relentless war on a new adversary: the KGB.

But when his one true love, April Rose, died at the hands of the Soviet terror machine, Bolan severed all ties with Establishment authority.

Now, after a lengthy lone-wolf struggle and much soul-searching, the Executioner has agreed to enter an "arm's-length" alliance with his government once more, reserving the right to pursue personal missions in his Everlasting War.

1

Atascadero, California

Gary Manning sighed as he sat in the sniper-hide and scanned the trees with his night-vision binoculars. "I hate babysitting jobs," he grumbled.

Mack Bolan silently agreed. He scanned the surrounding central California oak forest. Bodyguarding and babysitting were nearly synonymous in his book. You waited for the enemy to do something and then reacted to it. That was a recipe for disaster as the reaction often ended up happening after the damage was done. The man known as the Executioner was proactive. He believed in getting to the enemy before they could act.

"And babysitting billionaires?" Manning continued. "What's up with that?"

"He likes hunting." Bolan countered. "He can't be all bad."

Manning grunted noncommittally. The big Canadian was an avid hunter himself and had personally whiled away many a happy hour of his free time hunting the wild hogs that descended on the ranches, farms and wineries of California like a plague of porcine locusts every year. Their rooting created significant erosion damage to the hillsides every year. They voraciously ate any crop they came across.

As a result, pig-hunting season in California was a year-round proposition. Even with no restrictions on hunting them, the wild boar were winning.

Their population continued to increase. Their range continued to expand. Trophy-size hogs were everywhere.

So were men with rifles.

It was the perfect opportunity to stage a hunting "accident." The enemy, whoever they were, could have a hundred snipers in the area armed with high-powered rifles with high-powered optics; all sneaking through the woods wearing camouflage and no one in local law enforcement would bat an eye.

Bolan knew Manning would love to be hunting the big game but they had a job to do. He swung his sights onto the cabin. It was made of logs but what it was in reality was a three-story log mansion with guest wings, servants' quarters, a wine cellar and a fully equipped and domed astronomy observatory.

The net of the tennis court had been taken down and Philip Eckhart's helicopter was parked on it.

Eckhart was a billionaire, and three very real

attempts had recently been made on his life. Eckhart had decided to continue on with his anything but routine life, including his hunting trip. He had, however, stepped up security. Bolan knew that everything within a hundred-yard radius of the lodge was under video surveillance. The lodge grounds had a web of infrared laser motion detectors. Eight armed men wearing maroon Eckhart Endeavors windbreakers patrolled the grounds in two-man teams. Each team patrolled with a large guard dog. Another half-dozen security men were inside the house, checking security feeds and carrying pistols in concealment holsters.

Bolan frowned as Eckhart and a guest walked past a huge, open, brightly lit, second-story window. The man he watched was unremarkable to look at. He might be a billionaire but he was still wearing the same scuffed and stained khaki pants and flannel shirt from the dawn and dusk hunts of the day. Several of his companions had bagged pigs that were being roasted on huge spits in the backyard. Eckhart had held off on his own shots. It seemed he was waiting for a prize-winner.

A look of approval ghosted across Bolan's face as Eckhart's personal bodyguard shadowed the two men a few discreet steps behind. The man wasn't very tall but his shoulders were broad, he stood ramrod-straight and projected like he was a six footer. He wore khaki shorts and a company polo shirt that had been tailored to fit his physique. Unlike the rest of the security detail he made no effort to hide the Browning 9 mm automatic or the thirteen-inch khukri dagger he wore on his belt.

Eckhart had hired himself a Gurkha from Gurkha Security Limited.

The man missed nothing. His brows bunched with obvious concern as his charge walked past the window. It was clear the bodyguard had stopped trying to advise Eckhart on how to live to see another day. Instead the man had made himself Eckhart's shadow. The bodyguard gazed out the window in passing and Bolan could almost feel the former British soldier searching for him in the dark.

"Interesting," Manning remarked.

Phillip Eckhart was an interesting guy. He had grown up unremarkably in the San Luis Obispo area. Hunting and fishing had taken up most of his time to the detriment of most other things in his life. Two years of junior college had barely squeaked him into the California Polytechnical Institute, but once there he had excelled, graduating magna cum laude in computer science with a minor in archaeology, a subject that had remained a passion in his life. Eckhart had never invented anything. What he had excelled at was looking at something and figuring out a way to make it better. He'd started working in Silicon Valley for established companies. Eventually he started his own company, went public, sold it and was a millionaire at the age of thirty-five. He had taken the profits and started another company, and then another and another. Then he started buying other, well-established businesses and made them work better. Before long he was a billionaire. His umbrella company was Eckhart Endeavors. Through that he looked around, found things that interested him and engaged in fascinating endeavors that made stupendous profits. Wall Street constantly held its breath waiting to see what he would do next.

Now someone wanted him dead.

Bolan didn't find that surprising. One generally didn't become a billionaire without making enemies. Often, vast numbers of them. The one strange caveat to the situation was that Phillip Eckhart was the only known billionaire on the planet who also happened to be a genuinely nice guy.

The President of the United States was concerned by the threats to Eckhart's life. Eckhart was a friend and an important campaign contributor. Nonetheless Eckhart had refused the security services of the FBI, the CIA and the Secret Service, saying he could take care of himself. But the President was troubled. So was the CIA. Was Eckhart just being his eccentric self or was he involved in something he wanted to hide? The president had consulted Hal Brognola, Director of the Justice Department's Special Operations Group, who'd called in Bolan for a covert operation.

Phillip Eckhart's brain was a national treasure, and the country could not afford to lose him. Furthermore, if one of the wealthiest men on earth was really up to something ugly, the United States government needed to know about it. The men from Stony Man Farm had fanned out. Aaron "The Bear" Kurtzman and his team had begun their computer wizardry, looking into Eckhart's comings and goings while Bolan and Manning sat in a sweaty sniper-hide eating protein bars while the smell of roasted boar wafted up the hillside to torment them.

Eckhart's hired security wasn't bad, but if Bolan and Manning could sneak up within rifle range so could someone else, and the Executioner knew he could take Eckhart anytime he wanted to.

Manning spoke very quietly. A tiny LED was flashing on their security suite. "Motion, near Suspect One."

Bolan and Manning had spent the seventy-two hours before Eckhart arrived at the cabin mapping the valley and finding the best spots for an enemy to set up to kill Eckhart. They'd established a descending order of best possible points from which to launch an attack on the lodge. Bolan and Manning had rigged the sites with security. Suspect One was the prime spot in this neck of the woods for hunting billionaires. It gave a commanding view of the house and the grounds and was within five hundred yards, putting it well within range of a good rifle or a handheld rocket launcher. There was good cover and concealment and it offered several escape routes, one of which led to a glade that was wide enough to support a helicopter landing.

"Confirm motion," Bolan said.

The pigs had been setting off the motion sensors regularly.

"Motion confirmed on two sources." Manning looked up with a grim smile. "Sensors are picking up significant metal readings."

Unless they had eaten a hunter and his gear the one thing the wild boars of California didn't do was carry rifles, and something had tripped the motion sensors at Suspect One and was carrying a significant source of metal. Bolan took out his phone and pressed a preset number.

The Executioner watched as Eckhart stopped by a window and pulled out his phone. The billionaire stared at his phone for long moments while it rang. When he was off hunting, fishing, sailing or mountain climbing his personal secretary took all his calls. This was his personal phone. Only the people closest to him had access to this number. But, with the help of Kurtzman, Mack Bolan did, too. He watched Eckhart continue to stare at his phone. The screen was giving Eckhart no caller ID. The Executioner figured it was 50/50 whether he responded.

Eckhart suddenly flipped open the phone and answered brightly. "Eckhart!"

Bolan spoke quietly. "Mr. Eckhart, listen carefully. I'd like you to step away from the window."

Eckhart's face blanked for the barest instant and then he disappeared behind the three-foot beams of his log cabin mansion. "Who is this? What do you want?"

"I'm extra security for you. An attempt is about to made on your life. I would like you to very quietly pull your security teams, your staff and your guests into the house. I believe the enemy will have snipers and possible support weapons. Out in the open your men will be cut to pieces," the Executioner said.

"I have a sharpshooter in the observatory up top. How about he counter-snipes?"

Clearly Eckhart was thinking ahead but not far enough. "Pull him. The dome is a death trap. Your shooter will get one shot and then he'll be killed. You should have deployed him in the hills," Bolan said.

"I never thought of that, I—"

There was no time to debate tactics. "I gather you have a basement shelter that is fire and earthquake proof?"

"Yeah…"

"Get everyone in it," Bolan said.

"I'm not big on holing up. I'd rather keep my options flexible if I'm under attack," Eckhart said.

"I can't tell you what to do, Mr. Eckhart, but I would suggest you at least pull into the interior of the house, and if you see shots on the hillside try to hold your fire. I'm going to try to take the gunmen out, now, and you might hit me or a buddy of mine."

"What if they get past you?"

"The only way they'll get past us is if we're dead. At that point you're free to do whatever you like."

Eckhart was silent for a moment. "Sounds fair to me. Good luck!" he said.

"Thanks, and you." Bolan put his communication headset in place. "Stay on the line."

"You got it. Keep me advised," Eckhart replied.

Manning was smiling. "For a billionaire, he sounds like an okay Joe," he said.

Bolan muted his mike. "Yeah, let's keep the boy breathing."

Bolan and Manning pulled night-vision goggles down over their eyes and began their approach on Suspect One. The little redoubt had a pair of fallen trees that formed a natural berm, and between the two trunks there was ample room to aim a rifle from cover. At fifty yards Bolan and Manning each dropped to one knee. Two rifle barrels could be seen between the trunks.

The barrels had hoop-shaped muzzle breaks as big around as beer cans.

"Those are anti-materiel rifles," Manning whispered. "And bigger than fifty caliber."

"Two heavy weapons, that'll mean at least two spotters if not four. Make it a half dozen with a seventh as commander," Bolan said.

"These guys are serious," Manning said.

Bolan's blood went cold as the light-amplifying lenses of his goggles showed him a pair of lasers drawing green lines down toward the house. He keyed his headset. "Eckhart?" he whispered.

"Yeah," the billionaire responded.

"Where are you?"

"Just watching the football game with friends

while the pig finishes. Security is pulling back and my guests and I are all in the interior of the house like you said."

"Have everyone hit the floor! Now!" Bolan urged.

The hillside lit up like doomsday. Six-foot gouts of fire blasted from the muzzles of the two massive weapons. They fired and fired again, methodically. Splinters fountained off the side of the lodge as huge projectiles tore through the treated timber like tissue. Bolan could hear men and women screaming through his headset. The two massive weapons on the hillside jackhammered holes in the side of Eckhart's hunting retreat. Eckhart shouted in Bolan's earpiece. "We're under attack!"

"On it!" Bolan raced along the hillside with Manning silently taking his six. "I'm going to flank! Pin 'em down on my signal!" he told Manning.

Bolan split off and took the deer path that looped up behind the snipers' position. The antitank rifles kept punching holes through the lodge. Bolan came to the pocket on the hillside and found killers intent on business. Two men were crouched behind the gigantic rifles aiming through the firing slit formed by the fallen trunks. The optics attached to the weapons were impressive and appeared to include small targeting computers. Two more men were assisting with loading magazines into the smoking weapons. One more man, who was obviously in command, was watching the besieged lodge through binoculars.

The assassins should have had someone watching the back door.

"Now!" Bolan said.

Manning's automatic rifle roared to life and the gunners and loaders froze in shock as bullets ripped across the tree trunks. The commander sensed something behind him and started to turn.

Bolan spoke quietly. "Freeze."

The man dropped his binoculars on their strap and went for the Uzi slung by his side.

The Beretta 93-R machine pistol in Bolan's left hand walked a three-round burst up the commanding assassin's chest. The .50 caliber Desert Eagle in Bolan's right swung as the two loaders went for their submachine guns. They lost the tops of their heads for their trouble. The anti-materiel rifles were far too big to be wielded in close combat. The gunners dropped their weapons and went for their pistols. The Beretta trip-hammered one man's head apart and Bolan took two strides forward to point the smoking machine pistol between the surviving assassin's eyes. "Last chance. Take the pistol out with two fingers, left hand, and toss it away," he said.

The man stared down the muzzle of the Beretta and complied.

"How many more?" the Executioner asked.

The man gave the unwavering machine pistol a leery look but kept his mouth shut. Bolan chopped

the Desert Eagle down and clubbed the man uncon-
scious. "Manning, I have four hostiles down, one
prisoner."

"I see no more activity on the hill from my end.
You want me to come ahead?"

"No, go down and let Eckhart know the situation
seems to be contained. He'll probably be pretty
grateful. Try to pump him for anything useful before
local law enforcement show up and start asking
questions or his lawyers show up and start advising
him. I'll secure the prisoner. Then I'm going down
the trail to see if I can locate their extraction point.

"Copy that," Manning said.

2

San Luis Obispo, California

The Executioner connected his laptop computer to his secure satellite link and then leaned back on the hotel bed. He'd left Gary Manning with Eckhart for the last twenty-four hours to see if he could pick up any intel around the lodge while Kurtzman worked the angles from his end. Bolan had found an SUV on the back side of the hill. It had been rented in town under a false name. The prisoner wasn't talking so local law enforcement had handed him over to the FBI.

Bolan typed in a few codes and Aaron Kurtzman popped up on his screen in real time. "So what can you tell me about our buddy Eckhart?" Bolan asked.

Kurtzman grinned on the screen. "Well, Gary says his spit-roasted wild boar is fantastic. He's hot-tubbing with supermodels, drinking single malt Scotch and Eckhart calls him 'good buddy.'"

Bolan shook his head.

"He also says that Eckhart really is a hell of a guy. Real regular Joe, for a billionaire," Kurtzman added.

"That's what everyone seems to be saying," Bolan replied.

"I've been researching our man, and it seems to be true. For example, a few years back he invested in African diamond mines. He started dating a French actress who gave him the lecture about African blood diamonds and he completely divested himself of the business on his end and took a loss."

Bolan had to admit that was unusual for a captain of industry. "What else? There's got to be some dirt on the man."

"Well…he likes to date models."

"Big deal," Bolan said. "Anything else?"

"Well…he's always had a love affair with archaeology."

"Well, now we've got him." Bolan folded his arms across his chest decisively.

Kurtzman sighed. "I know. Hear me out. Amateur archaeology is his passion. The guy hands out grants like party favors to universities with red-hot archaeology departments. And if there's one real boondoggle in his life, one place where he makes bad business choices, it's archaeology. The man has thrown away some serious coin on far-flung digs and treasure hunts that went nowhere. Of course he can afford it, but we're talking about a genuine addiction for digging around in the sandbox."

Bolan considered the information. "Bring up his guest list at the hunting lodge again."

Kurtzman clicked keys and the names and photos popped onto Bolan's screen. He scanned them and pointed at a name. "Dr. Marcus Klein. Doctor of what?"

Kurtzman searched. "Professor of classical archaeology, UC Berkeley."

"Not your average great white hunter," Bolan said.

"No." Kurtzman's craggy brow furrowed. "He's a card-carrying member of PETA, actually."

"Something very intriguing must have made him ignore his scruples and attend a billionaire's pig hunt in rural California."

"He wants a grant? A lot of academics do a lot of things they're ashamed of to receive funding."

Bolan tapped another picture on his screen. "Who's the blonde?" She had long straight hair, arched eyebrows, full lips and big white teeth. She looked curvaceous and was wearing a pink argyle sweater and pin-striped pants. Stylish square eyeglasses completed her look. She had the fulsome, librarian seductress look going to the hilt. "She's not Eckhart's usual Euro-lanky ice-queen girlfriend."

Kurtzman grinned. He was a man who appreciated a woman with curves. "That is Nancy Rhynman. Double major in archaeology and linguistics. Specializing in ancient Greek studies on the one hand and primate body language on the other."

"Primate body language?"

"She wrote a thesis matching ape gestures, expressions and body language to humans. She speaks on the lecture circuit and gives corporate seminars on reading body language to help businesses get ahead."

"That's got to pay more than the ancient Greeks." Bolan's eyes narrowed. "What is Professor Klein's specialty?"

Kurtzman smiled as he saw where this was going. "The ancient Greeks."

"Eckhart probably wouldn't care about reading body language except as cocktail conversation. This Nancy gal is attractive but he already has a supermodel girlfriend. She's there for her archaeological expertise. So is Klein. I need you to find out what they're all up to," Bolan said.

The computer chimed. The Executioner clicked on Accept and a video inset of Gary Manning appeared. "Hello, boys!"

"What have you got on your end?' Bolan asked.

"Turns out the guys with the big guns were doing more than firing for effect. The weapons were Hungarian Gepard rifles. The M3 version, chambered for 14.5 mm Russian rounds. We're talking a thousand-grain bullet traveling at over three thousand feet per second. I surveyed the damage. You could put your fist through some of the holes they punched through that house."

Bolan had seen the weapons up close and didn't doubt it.

"And here's the real interesting thing," Manning continued. "They put a round through Eckhart's bedroom that hit his bed, his pillow actually, right on the side of the bed where he sleeps. In his private study his computer was smashed apart and the trajectory would have cut him in half if he'd been online. They put a round where he sits in his favorite chair in the TV room, one through the dining room that would have killed anyone sitting at the head of the table and another one would have taken him on the can in the master bedroom. These guys had intimate knowledge of Eckhart's place and had his usual stationary spots plotted in their firing computers. I've never seen an assassination attempt like this, but I'm telling you, it was slick."

The fact they knew the inside of Eckhart's house and the usual places he lurked implied he'd been betrayed from within and his enemies were willing to go to extraordinary lengths to kill him. "How's life at the lodge otherwise?" Bolan asked.

"Going swimmingly, actually. Phil and I are—"

"Phil?" Bolan inquired.

"Yeah, Phil. That's his name." Manning sounded vaguely offended. "Anyway, we all know Phil didn't want CIA spooks or FBI suits lurking in every corner of his life. But after last night he's pretty grateful and he seems to like me a whole lot." Manning was positively smug. "I just happen to have the news flash you've been waiting for."

"And what would that be?" Bolan asked.

"Eckhart's planning, how does he like to put it? An…endeavor."

Bolan and Kurtzman both smiled at the same time. "Would that be an archaeological endeavor?" Bolan asked.

Manning deflated as his thunder was stolen. "Yeah, how'd you know?"

"Skill and science. So where's our boy headed?" Kurtzman asked.

"Don't know. But he's hinting like it's a real roughing-it situation, and he implied it's outside North America. He mentioned mountains and unfriendly natives and asked if I knew how to ride a horse. The real interesting news is that Eckhart said he's hiring security for the endeavor, and we're talking mercs."

"So what did you say?" Bolan asked.

"I didn't have to say anything. He offered me the job of head of security."

"You took the job?" Bolan said.

"Naw, I wanted to, but I told him I couldn't do it. Told him I had other commitments. I did tell him I knew a guy who was reliable, not on the government payroll and needed a job." Manning gave Bolan a shit-eating grin over the link.

Bolan nodded. It was true, he didn't work for the United States government. It was truer to say he had a working relationship with it, though the lines got blurry sometimes even for him. "Nice work. You find out anything else?"

"Not too much. When he and I weren't flapping

our gums about the great outdoors Phil spent a lot of time in his private study with some professor guy and a bubbly blonde."

Bolan and Bear shot each other knowing looks.

Manning perked up. "Oh, and the Gurkha? I got his name. Lalbahadur Rai, and you were right, Striker. Phil hired him through Gurkha Security Limited, U.K. With that and his name we should be able to check his credentials, but I can tell you right now just by watching him. He's a badass."

Every Gurkha Bolan had ever met was. Pound for pound they were some of the toughest soldiers on earth. "How am I supposed to do the meet-and-greet with Eckhart?" he asked.

"Don't know your ultimate destination, but if you want the job, you'll meet him and the rest of his team in London. I chatted you up and he's excited to meet you. I also told him you were broke so he has a round-trip plane ticket, first class and spending money with your name on it if you'll come and give his endeavor a listen. Oh, and the job? It pays a thousand dollars a day, and he mentioned something about bonuses." Manning's face grew serious. "Oh, and one other thing."

Bolan instantly knew he wasn't going to like it. "What's that?"

"He's taking the attempts on his life seriously, but at the same time, he's not."

Bolan had seen this before in very powerful men. "This is a game to him."

"Guarding him isn't going to be easy." Manning leaned back in his chair. "What do you want me to tell him?"

Bolan glanced into his camera. "Bear?"

"Well I don't exactly like it." Kurtzman scratched his beard. "But this is exactly the kind of mysterious activity the president wanted investigated, that and keeping our billionaire's brain inside his skull are both going to be easier to do from the inside. It's your call, Striker, but I would say accept."

Bolan made his decision. "Gary, tell Phil I'm excited about this plan and I'm thankful to be a part of it."

THE EXECUTIONER WAS ON A PLANE to London when his laptop peeped at him. Bolan watched the codes scroll across the screen. Kurtzman was trying to contact him. Bolan keyed in his own codes and Kurtzman appeared on his screen. Bolan put his earbuds in place and opened an instant messaging window.

Kurtzman looked concerned. "We think we know your destination, at least generally," he said.

That was quick, Bolan typed. Where?

"Tajikistan. MI6 intercepted chatter."

Chatter from where? Bolan typed.

"From their agents in the People's Republic of China."

Bolan clicked some keys and brought up a map of Tajikistan. What's the gist of the chatter?

"Nothing conclusive. The only thing that is certain is that the Chinese know about Phillip Eckhart's endeavor. They knew where he was going before we did, and they seem to be keenly interested."

How would the Chinese find out?

"We don't know," Kurtzman said.

I can only think of one reason why China would care, Bolan typed.

Kurtzman nodded. "Heroin."

Bolan knew from hard experience that there were three major heroin production centers. One was in Latin America, based out of Mexico and Colombia. The second was Southeast Asia, with Myanmar being party central. The third was Southwest Asia, and Afghanistan was ground zero. Afghani heroin took two major overland routes. One was the Balkan route. Turkey was the anchor and from there it branched out through the Balkans to eastern and western Europe. The other path followed the ancient Silk Road to Russia, the Baltic states and other former Soviet republics. Tajikistan was a major gateway state of the Heroin Silk Route.

Bolan knew China had a new generation of billionaire venture capitalists who sailed the seas of international commerce like buccaneers, and Chinese Triads were still the biggest heroin merchants in the world. They got most of their product from Southeast Asia, but the new breed of Chinese businessmen and gangsters were nothing if not expansionist in outlook.

The U.S. invasion of Afghanistan and the toppling of the Taliban had done little to stop the Southwest Asian heroin trade, but many routes had been closed, many drug warlords had been toppled. The situation was in flux and there were vacuums to be filled. The Chinese underworld and the mostly off-the-leash venture capitalists were always looking for opportunity, and with the U.S. and coalition forces in a state of occupation in Afghanistan, having one of the richest and most influential men in America on your side could smooth smuggling matters considerably.

Kurtzman read Bolan's mind. "The Pentagon is thinking the same thing, but I don't buy it. A man who willingly lost millions in the gem trade over his moral issues just isn't the guy who's going to set himself up in the international trade in junk. He doesn't need the money. I just don't buy it."

Bolan had to admit that he didn't, either. He'd only spoken to Eckhart for a few seconds but the vibe was wrong, and if Gary Manning said Eckhart seemed to be a stand-up guy, Bolan was willing to trust the big Canadian's instincts.

Okay, lets get back to archaeology. Dr. Klein and Nancy Rhynman both specialize in the ancient Greeks. Why would Eckhart be consulting them about Tajikistan? Bolan glanced at the map on his computer screen. That's three thousand miles off course.

"It is a conundrum," Kurtzman admitted. "You're

just going to have to take the meeting and then you can tell me."

You have gear in place for me? Bolan typed.

"A man is going to meet you when you get off the plane and give you a key. Take a cab from the airport. There's a storage facility a few miles down the road. You'll have a map, the key and the account number. The storage unit has a Land Rover parked in it and everything you asked for and everything else we could think of on our end."

Thanks, Bear, Bolan typed. Anything else pertinent?

"Yeah, I took Manning's info and found our Gurkha. Lalbahadur Rai reached the rank of havildar, which is the equivalent of sergeant in the British Army. He served with the British Brigade of Gurkhas C Company, Second Battalion, Parachute Regiment. He served with distinction and when it came time to re-enlist he opted to go to work in the private sector for the firm Global Risks. He served from 2005 through 2007. What he did there is company classified. We can find out but it will take a dedicated hack and some time."

That's enough to start with. With any luck he and I are going to end up being allies, Bolan typed.

"So you have a plan?"

Yeah. Bolan checked his watch. Touchdown in London was another two hours away. I'm going to take a nap, eat the in-flight breakfast and then take a meeting with a billionaire.

3

London

The Endeavor team meeting was in ten minutes. Bolan had gotten off the plane, ignored the man in chauffeur livery holding the sign that read Matt Cooper, met his Stony Man contact, gotten a cab, gone to the storage facility and geared up. Phillip Eckhart was the kind of man who did everything right. He didn't go in for gold-plated toothbrushes and diamond-studded toilets, but he did insist on quality. The Stafford Hotel was not the fanciest in London, it lacked amenities like an in-house spa and gym and the rooms were not palatial. What the Stafford had was class and many travelers considered it the best hotel in London. The eighty-room Edwardian town house was centrally located on a secluded street with its own private access to Green Park and it had service in spades.

Eckhart had been mildly surprised when the Executioner had walked into the bar and introduced

himself as Matt Cooper. He had looked Bolan up
and down like he might examine a new company's
prospectus and apparently liked what he saw. He
told Bolan that his good buddy from Canada had
recommended him highly and that was good enough
for him. He'd handed Bolan a folder full of files and
asked him to peruse it at his leisure before the private
dinner meeting later.

Back in his room Bolan examined each personnel file, scanned it and then e-mailed it to the Farm.
Phillip Eckhart had hired himself his own private
army. The men were from all corners of the globe,
but so were Eckhart's business contacts, and he had
told Bolan each man came highly recommended
from one respected source or another. Just as Bolan
had himself.

Bolan ran the files a second time. Each man had
served in private military forces. If you had served
in your national army with distinction, had a useful
military specialty, or had the magic "Special Forces"
moniker attached to your record you could earn,
double, triple or even quadruple pay compared to
regular military service. The opportunity to safe-
guard convoys, local royalty and political bigwigs,
or bodyguard your occasional billionaire, could
bring perks and social and business contacts beyond
the wildest dreams of a regular serviceman.

Bolan flipped through the files. Each one
included a photo, a brief of each man's service
record and his nickname written over his picture.

Vivian "Viv" Blackpool was an Englishman from the famous beach town of the same name. He had served in Her Majesty's Royal Artillery. The file said he had been a forward observation officer. That meant his job was to creep behind enemy lines, find the enemy, radio back to the artillery and ground attack fighters and rain hell down on them. He'd won the Conspicuous Gallantry Cross in Afghanistan. He had a steel-wool-tight white man's afro and a jaw like a lantern. Eckhart had written *Scout* on his file.

Gobun Yagi had been a rugby player for team Kobe Steel. He'd served with Japanese 1st Airborne and been deployed to Iraq. Japan didn't have official Special Forces but Yagi had qualified for the Central Readiness Force that was their closest equivalent. He was deeply tanned, had a shag haircut with strands of silver in it and he was grinning good-naturedly in his file photo. Eckhart had written C^3 over Yagi's photo with a red pen. C cubed stood for communications, command and control. Bolan knew that meant Yagi would be trained in battlefield communications with radios, computers and satellites. Bolan noted the warrior had also been a hand-to-hand combat instructor.

The big American flipped to the next file.

Yuli Simutenkov was a Russian who had served in his nation's 10th Mountain Brigade. He had done two tours in Chechnya then deserted. Bolan had a hard time blaming him. He had then managed to smuggle himself to Paris and joined the French Foreign Legion. Eckhart had used a yellow highlighter to emphasize that while Simutenkov was ethnically Russian he had been born in the city of Shaymak, which just happened to be the most eastern city in Tajikistan. His language proficiencies were also highlighted. He spoke Russian and his native Tajik as well as Kyrg, Arabic, Mandarin, English and French. He was blue-eyed, blunt-featured and had taken up the Russian military in-the-field habit of shaving his head and then letting his skull and beard stubble grow to same length. In his photo he was smiling in a not particularly friendly fashion with a hand-rolled cigarette dangling out of his mouth. Some of his teeth were gold, some were silver and some were missing. Eckhart had written *Interpreter* over his picture.

Bolan raised an eyebrow at the next photo. You didn't hear about Hungarian mercenaries very often, but Zoltan "ZJ" Juhasz was a combat engineer who had served attached to the Hungarian 88th Rapid Reaction Force in Afghanistan. With his wavy black hair, arched eyebrows and Vandyke beard he looked like a Napoleonic Hussar, or Satan, or maybe just a man from Eastern Europe who enjoyed playing with explosives a little too much. Eckhart had written *Demo Man!!!* over the Hungarian's head.

Bolan turned the page. Gilad Shlomo Gideon, or "Giddy" had served ten years with the Israeli Field Intelligence Corps. They were tasked with collecting combat intelligence in real time during battle, which meant that there was probably very little in the way of modern warfare the man had not seen or done. He was a wiry-looking guy with curls even tighter than Blackpool's. *Medic* was scrawled above his picture. Bolan frowned. Interrogation was written below it. As a battlefield intelligence man Bolan suspected Gilad was skilled in keeping the wounded alive long enough to give up the goods.

He flipped to the next page. Pieter Van's blond hair was almost white and his fair skin turned to saddle leather by years of fighting under the African sun. He had been a South African SAS commando and his resume read like a travelogue of every African trouble spot in the last twenty years. He'd worked security for several diamond consortiums in Africa that was undoubtedly where Eckhart had met him. *Sniper* was written and underlined on his photo.

Bolan turned over another wild card. Evo Solomon "Waqa" Waqa was Fijian. The man had a head like a block of granite and his hair was a series of two-inch, cone-shaped spikes that stuck up out of his head in remarkable imitation of Bart Simpson. Bolan noted his career highlights. He had been a member of Fiji's infamous "Zulu" company counterrevolutionary specialists. The unit had been disbanded after elements of it had mutinied during the 2000 coup. Waqa had survived the purge and gone on to serve with the United Nations peace-keeping forces in East Timor. Over his name Eckhart had

written *Rai recommended,* and Bolan recalled that
five hundred Fijians had served or were serving with
the Global Risks group in Iraq along with a similar
number of Nepalese. Bolan doubted a Gurkha
rifleman would recommend any non-Nepalese who
couldn't pass muster.

The last man was an American. He had blond hair
and a blinding smile. He was grinning out of an
American military ID photo and just from his neck
and shoulders alone Bolan could tell the man had
spent many hours pushing heavy iron in the gym.
Roy Blair was 3rd Ranger Battalion. He'd been in
Afghanistan then redeployed to Iraq. He then opted
not to reenlist but had stayed in Iraq and gone to
work for a private security company. *Pig* was written
over his photo. That was Ranger-speak. There were
two kinds of Rangers. "Maggots" were riflemen and
"Pigs" were in the weapons squad. Roy Blair would
know his way around machine guns, recoilless rifles,
and antitank and antiaircraft weapons.

Bolan grunted in thin amusement at the last file.
It had one word typed in quotes, center-spaced.

Cooper?

There was a hand-drawn smiley face beneath it.

There was another page that had a table with each
man's name and then a number of specialties
checked off. Each man could ride a horse. Each man
had qualified as expert or his national army's equivalent with a rifle. Each man had passed courses in
mountaineering and orienteering. Some men had

specialty footnotes. Waqa, of all people, was a cook. Pieter could fly a helicopter and both Blackpool and Yuli could drive semis. Zoltan had *Wrangler* checked off by his name so the Hungarian probably knew something about the care and feeding of horses and he had been a Hungarian armed forces fencing champion. Roy Blair had attended the Defense Language Institute between deployments and learned basic Arabic. Yagi had done the Japanese equivalent and spoke Mandarin. Not surprisingly for a combat intelligence man in the Middle East, Giddy spoke Arabic as well as Farsi. Bolan's line was empty so he checked off a few boxes that applied. He left out a lot. He'd demonstrate those abilities when and if the time came, and he'd give Eckhart his impressions after he'd had face time with each man.

Bolan closed the folder and grunted to himself. Eckhart had his own private little Foreign Legion and Bolan had joined it.

The Executioner checked the loads in his sound-suppressed Beretta 93-R. It was a .22 caliber conversion and had twenty-five rounds in the magazine plus one in chamber. He placed it in a shoulder holster under his left arm and four spare magazines rode under his right. Bolan pulled on a black leather jacket and went downstairs to the hotel's private meeting room.

Sitting around the conference table were a billionaire, his bodyguard, a hot blonde and eight very dangerous men.

Eckhart gave Bolan a friendly wave and gestured at the one empty chair. "Coop! Glad you could join us. Take a seat."

Bolan handed the file back to Eckhart and took the offered chair. He nodded to the Fijian and Hungarian sitting to either side of him.

Eckhart called the group to attention. "Gentlemen, let's get started. First off, you will all find a nondisclosure contract in front of you, which I will require you to sign if you want to attend the rest of this meeting. If you don't wish to sign, I'll have to ask you to leave immediately."

This was met by some muttering but Eckhart waved it away dismissively. "However, your rent here at the Stafford is paid 'til the end of the week, you have an open tab at the bar and your return tickets are open-ended. Thank you for coming."

The soldiers made mollified noises.

Eckhart's face became serious. "If you sign, stay and afterward do not wish to participate, you may leave. However, if you sign and then break the nondisclosure contract and talk about what is discussed in this room outside of the Endeavor Team here assembled, you will be subject to the kind of lawyers and lawsuits only a billionaire can bring on. And, short of hiring hit men, I will use every legal, political and business contact I have to shit on you for the rest of your lives. I strongly urge you to think about that before you sign."

No one had to think about it. A couple of the men

made a pretense of flipping through the pages of legalese but everyone quickly signed. Rai collected the contracts and put them in a folder.

"Good." Eckhart rapped his knuckles on the table and on cue two of the hotel staff staggered in carrying buckets of beers from around the world on ice. The arrival was met with cheers. Bolan smiled inwardly. Alcohol had been part of successful soldier recruitment since the Renaissance. Beers were passed around the table and Bolan picked himself out a Guinness.

"Gentlemen, may I introduce Nancy Rhynman," Eckhart continued. "She'll be part of our team."

A chorus of whistles and catcalls greeted the news. Bolan noted Rhynman blushed slightly and smiled at the barrage of lewd suggestions but she didn't seem intimidated.

"Most of you have probably heard of me," Eckhart said.

This was met with some pointed comments that Eckhart ignored. "And as you may have heard every once in a while I go off on an endeavor in the name of science. Africa, the Amazon, Southeast Asia, I've had a few adventures around the globe and been on a few boondoggles." Eckhart eyed the assembled soldiers wryly. "As I suspect as most of you."

The comment was met by grunts of agreement.

Eckhart spread his hands in mock helplessness. "Well, I'm off on another one! And it's going to require stepped-up security. That's where you men come in."

Waqa leaned back and frowned impatiently. The chair creaked ominously beneath his massive frame. "What's the job, brah?"

Eckhart nodded to Rhynman. "Nancy?"

The soldiers sighed as she rose and they approved of the way her lightweight wool pants clung to her curves. She clicked a remote control and a projector showed a map on the wall that stretched from Spain to Hong Kong. "This is the modern world." She clicked the remote again and nearly all the cities disappeared. "This is the ancient world." Nancy clicked her remote again. "And this was the world of Alexander the Great."

The map lit up in highlight from Mount Olympus in Western Greece to the Himalayas.

"As you may or may not remember from your school days, Alexander and his army conquered all the way across what is today modern Turkey, Iraq and Iran. His conquests spread from—"

"Jesus, here comes the History Channel." Blair's boots thudded on top of the table as he rocked back in his chair. "Can't you make this more entertaining?"

"Take off your clothes!" Waqa suggested.

Eckhart held up his hand. "Guys …"

"Da!" Yuli produced a one-hundred-pound note. "Dance! Dance on table!"

Blair spread his feet on the table. "Lap dance!"

Eckhart might have been a billionaire and a captain of industry but he suddenly found himself in a room full of rowdy soldiers whose respect he hadn't earned. "Gentlemen, I—" he stammered.

"Show us your tits!" Waqa shouted.

Again Bolan noticed that Nancy wasn't scared, embarrassed or intimidated. She was quietly and coldly becoming furious. He saw an opportunity to get on her good side. He picked his victim. His voice cut through the cacophony of sexual harassment and hilarity.

"Yo, Waqa."

Waqa grinned and cracked himself another beer. "Yeah, brah?"

"I've got no money in my pocket, a bucket of beer I haven't finished and I need this job." The room went dead silent as Bolan's arctic blue eyes bored into Waqa's. His voice was as serious as the grave. "Don't screw this up."

The Fijian was clearly not used to being challenged but he found himself taken aback and blinking at Bolan's glacial gaze. "Shit, I'm just having some fun," he said.

Pieter Van spoke like the elder statesman of the group. "Enough of this *kak.* I too need a job, and I would like to hear what Miss Rhynman and Mr. Eckhart have to say." He spoke with the authority of a veteran commander. "I believe those who do not need the work already know the location of the door."

An awkward silence fell across the table.

Bolan noticed Rhynman staring at him. She

wasn't beaming in gratitude. She was taking mental notes. Bolan reminded himself that she was a body language expert as well as an archaeologist. He suspected she would be writing assessments of every soldier around the table to add to Eckhart's personnel files.

"So, Miss Rhynman," Pieter said. "Alexander the Great?"

"Let me summarize," Rhynman said. "Alexander the Great conquered a big chunk of real estate. Wherever he went he built Alexandrias, cities that bore his name, and he left generals and trusted companions to command and rule from them. To this day ancient Greek artifacts and even ruins turn up all over this territory from Egypt to India."

The men were beginning to roll their eyes and look at one another in disbelief. The blonde scholar looked around the room and could tell she was losing her audience. "What we are looking for is the Citadel of Hades," she announced.

That got everyone's attention.

"What the fuck?" Blair asked.

"We're looking for a hidden fortress. Farther east than any historian believes Alexander ever got. A lost citadel gentlemen, perhaps the last great classical archaeological find that remains undiscovered. Right on par with the pyramids of Egypt and the Coliseum of Rome."

The soldiers looked at one another and didn't know what to think.

Eckhart began his pitch. "Men, I've recently been doing some investing in western Asia. Wherever I am I'm always looking into the local antiquities market. I was in Tajikistan when some Greek writings literally fell into my hands. The seller was a local tribesman who had no idea what he had. When I began to suspect what I'd found I contacted Nancy, and she contacted scholars she knew in the field, and it appears to be genuine."

Giddy peered at Eckhart with genuine interest. "What did you find?"

Eckhart was positively smug. "The writings of Gorgidas of Thebes."

Yagi spoke for the first time. "I do not know what that means."

Rhynman took over. "Alexander wanted to be remembered. He wanted his accomplishments to be heralded throughout the ages. So he took Greek scribes along with him wherever he went. The scribe these writings are attributed to, Gorgidas, wasn't very famous as Greek writers went. Much of his writing was considered trivial and catalogued day-to-day goings-on in camp and on the march. He was almost a glorified accountant. But for some reason Alexander took Gorgidas with him when he went on a secret journey to the Citadel of Hades, and Gorgidas recorded the trip."

"Citadel of Hades," Bolan said, adopting a relaxed pose. "I never went to college but doesn't that mean Citadel of Hell?"

Rhynman shook her head. "Close, but not quite. Hades is the Underworld, but in Greek mythology it's a dark and gloomy place rather than the Christian Hell. Gorgidas speaks of 'a house of weeping columns with walls of glittering stone' in his writings."

Bolan took the obvious leap of logic. "So it's a cave."

"Yes." Nancy Rhynman favored Bolan with a smile. "In the metaphor of the day a Citadel of Hades would imply a subterranean fortress. Weeping columns could mean stalagmites and stalactites, and walls of glittering stone most likely would refer to quartz formations that happen to be rampant in our target area. Many cultures throughout the ages have taken natural-occurring cave complexes and dug citadels and fortresses within them. Those of you who have fought in Afghanistan know the entire region is riddled with caverns. We have no idea how old this citadel might be, but it was most likely built or inherited by the Persian Achaemenid Empire, and when Alexander conquered them it appears he received access to it. Think of it, a hidden citadel, and secret refuge, a—"

"A fortress of solitude?" Blackpool suggested. "Has he got one at the North Pole, too, then?"

Rhynman smiled but her eyes went cold. "'Fortress of solitude' might not be a bad metaphor. If the Citadel is there it's way off the beaten path. Nothing in the way of agriculture or civilization was anywhere close. Resources in the Pamir Mountains are scarce. It might well be a fortress of solitude, Mr. Blackpool. A place where people were sent into exile or went to hide during wars of succession." Rhynman leaned slightly forward, fixed Blackpool in place with her eyes and raised one eyebrow in challenge. "Or it might also be a place to store unimaginable wealth."

Waqa leaned forward. "You're talking like treasure and shit."

"Yes, Mr. Waqa," Rhynman confirmed. "Treasure and shit. Wherever Alexander went he demanded tribute, and the Persian Empire of Darius was the richest in the world. Much of the vast wealth that Alexander took was never accounted for. Undoubtedly a great deal was stolen by his successors after his death and the breakup of his empire. But there is enough accounting in the archaeological record to suggest that huge amounts of it were hidden and only Alexander and a few of his closest confederates knew its whereabouts.

"Alexander died suddenly without settling his affairs. The fact is there is the possibility of gold, silver, gems and jewels being stored in this location by the ton. Not to mention a priceless archaeological trove of writings, sculptures, tools, weapons and fabrics—with luck all perfectly preserved in the subterranean environment. The Tajik government will most likely try to claim most of it as natural heritage." Nancy Rhynman's smile became predatory.

"But our employer pretty much has the ability to buy Tajikistan lock, stock and barrel."

This was met by harsh, renewed laughter.

Rhynman waited for it to die down. "And even if there's nothing there but bare rock, just finding the Citadel will be the greatest archaeological discovery of this century. You'll all be famous. All the news agencies will pay to interview you. We're talking TV, radio, Internet and printed press. All of you will be heroes in your native countries. There will be movie rights, book rights, you name it, and Mr. Eckhart is willing to extend to you free financial advisement to make the most of all opportunities that you may accrue from this endeavor."

There was silence around the table.

Eckhart filled it. "And if all we find is scorpions and dirt, I'm still paying a thousand dollars a day." The billionaire smiled. "So, who's in?"

4

The reactions to Alexander the Great's lost Citadel in Tajikistan had ranged from rude noises and boredom to expressions of pity and disbelief. On the other hand every man in the room, no matter what country he was from, had read about Phillip Eckhart in magazines and seen him on television. He was a billionaire and he was paying a thousand dollars a day…plus bonuses. Every man was in.

The meeting adjourned until noon the next day and the ex-soldiers went off to seek amusement. Blair, Blackpool and Waqa spontaneously wandered off into the London night to look for adventure. Yagi accosted one of the hotel staff and by the way the concierge was blushing and stammering it was pretty clear he was inquiring where a man with a thousand pounds in his pocket went to get laid. Gilad was leaning in and listening intently. Zoltan plunked himself down beside Rhynman and began chatting her up. Yuli wandered off by himself, riffing through his wad of pound notes and undoubtedly calculating some personal endeavor of his own.

Bolan grabbed a bottle of beer and made for his room. He had some very interesting information for Kurtzman. Pieter sidled up to Bolan as he waited for the elevator and spoke quietly. "*Hie,* Coop. Tell me, you seem solid. What do you think of all this Alexander the Great, Tomb Raider *kak?*"

Bolan snorted. "Don't know, don't have an opinion."

The South African gazed at Bolan in open suspicion. "Truly?"

"Okay. For a thousand bucks a day we're not getting paid to have an opinion. That's what I think." Bolan shrugged. "They say Alexander got all the way to India. Tajikistan was part of the Silk Road. It went all the way to Greece back in the day."

"I attended secondary school, too. But do you believe it?"

"Do you?" Bolan gazed at the South African shrewdly. "I get the impression you know this Eckhart guy pretty well. You tell me what you think."

"You're a canny one. I do know him. Never met anyone shrewder in business, either, but…"

"But?" Bolan prompted.

"But as his security chief I saw him turn his back on enough diamonds to cover a beach like sand. This endeavor. This is passion. This is obsession. A pipe dream. And I'll tell you, Cooper. I'm old now. I'll be fifty before this thing is done. Too old to be chasing dreams."

"Thousand dollars a day," Bolan reminded him.

The mercenary suddenly flashed his teeth. "It's magic!"

Bolan found himself liking the man. "Tell you what, Piet. You seem solid, too." Bolan went with his instincts and stuck out his hand. "I'll watch your back if you watch mine."

Piet pumped Bolan's hand. "Gladly." He clapped his hand on Bolan's shoulder. "You're a good man, Coop. For a Yank. Let's hit the bar."

"Gimme a few minutes. I want to let some people know I won't be home for a while," Bolan said.

"Meet you then. But you will forgive me if I start without you."

"I'll catch up."

Piet snorted. "You'll try."

Zoltan sauntered up, grinning through his mustache. "Do you boys mind if I join you?"

Piet regarded the Hungarian bemusedly. "No luck with Miss Rhynman, then?"

ZJ frowned. "The trip will be long, there will be sleeping bags under the stars and I am a very charming man." He twirled his mustache and resumed grinning. "The groundwork has been laid."

"Well since you're not getting laid tonight, sure, join us," Bolan said.

ZJ gave Bolan a wounded look but followed Piet toward the bar.

Before Bolan got in the elevator he gave Eckhart a call to let him know he was dropping by his room. He stared at the phone for several moments as no one picked up. He let it ring and go to voice mail then hung up and put the phone back in his pocket. He headed to Eckhart's floor and came out whistling as if he hadn't a care in the world. A stout woman from housekeeping with her red hair in a bun was outside of Eckhart's door with a cart of linens. She was wiping the brass knob and hinges on the antique door. Bolan waggled the bottle of beer in his hand. "Eckhart around?"

The woman spoke with a thick accent Bolan couldn't identify. "No. Mr. Eckhart is out," she said.

"Oh." Bolan walked on by. He brought his beer up to his chest and gave it three violent shakes as he heard footsteps behind him. He spun and ducked. He fire-hosed beer into the woman's face as her stun gun sparked. The arcing prongs missed Bolan's throat by inches as he ripped his Beretta free. As the woman blinked and coughed froth he chopped the butt into the side of her head. She fell to the carpet. Bolan kicked in Eckhart's door.

It took him but a heartbeat to read the scene.

The window was open and a rope ladder had been deployed. Eckhart was facedown on the bed. A big man with a shaved head had his knee in the billionaire's back and was hog-tying him. Eckhart had the shuddering, glazed, just-electrocuted look about him. Lalbahadur Rai was on one knee with two

Taser probes in his chest. His pistol was on the floor but his knife was held in one white-knuckled hand. His body twisted as he struggled to rise against the current coursing through his body. The second man was snarling as he held the button down on the juice to force the Gurkha down. Both men gaped at the intruder in shock. Bolan extended his pistol and fired.

The man on Eckhart gagged as three .22 caliber hollow-point bullets opened his throat. He fell to the floor as Bolan spun on the other man. He dropped his Taser and slapped leather for the pistol on his belt with admirable alacrity but Bolan's tri-burst punched a divot in the notch between the man's collarbones. Blood erupted out of the hollow of his throat as he choked and fell.

The big American quickly swept the room and pulled up the ladder. The newly hired team had all exchanged numbers at the meeting. Bolan called Piet and the South African answered on the first ring. "Coop. What is it?"

"Someone just made an attempt on Eckhart. Grab ZJ and get up here. There's a woman down in the hall. She's one of them. Bring her in."

"Coming!" The line clicked off. Bolan flicked open his switchblade and used the spear blade to cut the plastic restraints holding Eckhart. "You all right?"

Eckhart gave Bolan a shaky smile.

Eckhart was all right. Bolan went to Rai. The Gurkha was twitching but he had ripped the probes from his chest and retrieved his pistol. "You all right?"

"I am all right, Cooper." Rai looked more chagrined than injured. "Thank you for coming."

"No problem."

Piet called from the hallway. "Coop!"

Bolan shouted back. "Clear!"

Piet came in warily holding a ten-inch chef's knife he had acquired from the hotel kitchen. "Everyone all right?"

"Yeah," Bolan said.

ZJ dragged in the big woman. She could barely stand and he held a meat cleaver to her throat. He shoved her roughly to the bed. Bolan went to a small black case on the bed. It was open and inside there were more plastic restraints, a second stun gun as well as an open medical kit with a pair of syringes.

Eckhart sat down shakily. "That's the fourth goddamn attempt on my life in as many weeks."

Bolan took out a syringe and a length of rubber tubing fell out with it. He expressed a drop of liquid onto his fingertip and rubbed it onto his gums. "This is heroin. This wasn't a hit. It was a kidnapping. They were going to Taser you, hog-tie you and send you to your happy place." Bolan glanced at the rolled-up rope ladder. "Then they were going to take you for a ride."

Eckhart struggled for something clever to say and failed. "Well…shit."

"Yeah." Bolan nodded at Piet and ZJ. "Take their guns. Go check on Nancy. Do it now."

Piet and ZJ stripped the two dead men of their handguns, checked the loads and ran from the room.

Bolan stared at the woman. She lay back on the bed clutching her head. "Mr. Eckhart, we can talk to her, we can call the authorities, or you can put in the call to someone you know."

Eckhart considered the options. "I have friends in London who can make sure this never reaches the news, and make sure she gets to meet members of MI6."

Bolan tossed his phone onto the bed beside Eckhart. "Make the call."

ECKHART WAS HOLDING COURT in the conference room. It was early morning, but men in long coats had come in the night and taken the false house-keeper away and by now everyone knew Eckhart had been attacked. The assembled men had been told to go out and have a good time, but they had been paid and their employer had been hit. That meant it was on their watch and all of the mercs were angry and appalled.

"Men," Eckhart said, nodding, "last night, we got hit."

This was met by angry muttering. Eckhart waved it away. "But our mission continues, and though we walk through the valley of the shadow of death, we shall not go into that dark vale unarmed."

Eckhart pulled a rifle from its foam packing. "Behold the Barret M468."

The assembled soldiers leaned forward with interest. Weaponcraft was far more up their alley than classical Greece. Eckhart continued. "Chambered in the Remington 6.8 mm round it has fifty percent more stopping power than an M-16 and up to 800 meters in range. We aren't looking for trouble, but if trouble finds us? It's in serious fucking trouble."

Laughs rolled around the room. In most situations soldiers would sneer at a civilian talking like this, but Eckhart's genuine enthusiasm for his endeavor was infectious and he was paying big money and showering them with toys. Bolan made a mental note that as well as being passionate about hunting, fishing, archaeology and European super-models, Phillip Eckhart was a gun nut. Bolan raised his hand.

Eckhart smiled and set the rifle down. "Yeah, Coop?"

"We expecting aerial resupply?"

Eckhart frowned. "Uh…no. I'll have helicopters in the closest cities to our route in Tajikistan to call in case of we need emergency extraction, but other than that we are under the radar and will be left to our own devices on the trail. Once we find the site, we establish provenance, contact the Tajik government and turn it into an international dig. Why do you ask?"

"Because if we do get in a firefight, our only way to restock our ammo will be to borrow, buy, steal or strip it off the dead. Every country in that part of the world uses Russian equipment, mostly old and thirty caliber. For this trip you're going to want AKs. I'd go with the 103 models. They have a mounting plate for the latest optical sights but can still feed off some tribesman's fifty-year old heirloom AK-47 magazine."

Eckhart stared down at the gleaming Barret like a boy on Christmas morning who had just been told to rewrap his present and send it back to the North Pole in exchange for a lump of coal.

Yuli raised his hand and grunted at Bolan reluctantly. "Cooper is correct. You will be wanting Kalashnikovs. Machine guns, handguns, support weapons. All should be Russian as well. You say you do not expect trouble? I say expect it. Besides attempt on your life? Tajikistan—whole country is…" English was Yuli's fifth language and he sought a metaphor. He grinned unpleasantly as he found one. "Dodge City."

Eckhart rolled with the punches. "Duly noted! This is exactly why I called this meeting. I need your input." He suddenly stabbed a finger at Bolan. "And you just got promoted to procurement. Make me a list."

Bolan leaned back in his chair. "Can do."

Blackpool spoke in a stage whisper across the table. "He's a cheeky monkey, this Coop…but I like him!"

More laughter rolled around the room.

Eckhart held up his hands for quiet. "I have a friend who has an estate in the Lake District. Once we have all our weapons, gear and kit we'll spend a few days out there doing familiarization. Gentlemen, I want to be in Dushanbe within the week."

5

Assault rifles cracked and snapped like strings of popcorn. Empty beer cans flew, danced and crumpled as the Russian automatic rifles Bolan had requisitioned wreaked havoc.

The men practicing with them were very good.

Eckhart had procured everything on Bolan's shopping list. Pieter Van's marksmanship was just short of inhuman so Bolan had requested a Dragunov sniper rifle for the South African and himself. Blair and Yuli were both grenadier qualified so their AK-103s had 30 mm GP-30 grenade launchers mounted beneath their barrels and every weapon had an optical sight. Eckhart had raised a bemused eyebrow but Bolan had insisted on bayonets for every weapon. Bolan had been in tunnel complexes before where it had come down to cold steel in the dark.

As far as handguns went Bolan wasn't a big fan of the Russian Makarov. It was too big to be a pocket pistol and too small and underpowered to be a service weapon. But it was standard issue in every former Soviet republic from the Caspian Sea to Mongolia. Every man on Team Endeavor was carrying one. Bolan had quietly put in a separate request for a PB silenced model, a Stetchkin machine pistol and an R-92 compact revolver with an ankle holster all in the same caliber.

The Executioner had also made a small but succinct list of explosives and support weapons.

Eckhart had delivered on all the goods with glee. The billionaire was standing at the far edge of the firing line. Bolan laid down his rifle and spent a few moments watching Eckhart shoot. The man had gotten over his high-tech weapon obsession and was putting his AK through its paces. It was clear he was an accomplished hunter. He was knocking down beer cans under Rai's sternly approving supervision.

Bolan smiled as Nancy Rhynman walked onto the range. She was dressed for effect in a pink angora sweater and black pants. She put on a pair of ear protectors as she walked onto the line but she wasn't carrying any gear. Rhynman watched the men shoot with an inscrutable look on her face. She was taking notes again.

Bolan walked over to her. "You're not shooting?"

Her nose wrinkled. "I don't believe in guns."

Bolan shrugged. "I don't believe in Santa Claus, but there's usually a little something for me under the tree most years."

One corner of Rhynman's mouth quirked. "You're a very interesting man, Mr. Cooper."

Bolan didn't bother to deny it. "It's true."

The other corner of her mouth reluctantly moved upward. "You know I can read every man on this firing line except you."

"Yeah?" Bolan lifted his chin at the team. "So what do you make of them?"

Rhynman warmed up to her area of expertise. "Blackpool is as solid as a rock, though there's some very deep sadness there," she said.

Bolan decided to play one of the cards that Kurtzman had given him. "His wife died of cancer a year ago. It ate up the family finances. He really needs this job."

She gave Bolan a long look. He gazed at the Fijian. "What about Waqa?"

"He's a great big kid who never grew up."

Bolan agreed. "Yagi?"

"He's actually very outgoing, but he's a little nervous in this company. He feels like he got hired for his technical abilities rather than as a soldier. I'm worried that he might try to overcompensate for it to prove himself."

Bolan looked at the little Hungarian. "And ZJ?"

Nancy snorted. "Definitely overcompensating for something."

Bolan took a long look at his fellow American merc. "And Blair?"

"At first I thought he was compensating for something as well." She shook her head at the ex-Ranger. "Now I think he's just Maximum Blair, 24/7. A real Type A personality type of guy."

Bolan nodded at the Israeli. "Gilad?"

"He comes off as Mr. Happy-Go-Lucky, but he's deep. Very deep."

"And Piet?" Bolan asked.

"The only reason he's still soldiering is because he doesn't know what else to do. He's past it and he knows it."

Bolan had to admit the woman was good. He watched the Russian as he blasted beer cans into oblivion with deliberate three round bursts. "Yuli?"

Nancy's eyes narrowed. "Borderline sociopath."

Bolan glanced at the Gurkha. "Rai?"

"He's a Nepalese samurai. Totally focused. Totally loyal."

"How about our employer?" Bolan queried.

"Phil?" She rolled her eyes. "What you see is what you get. He's like Waqa, except driven, and that puts six more zeroes in his bank account than most people have. He's just your typical impassioned boy billionaire."

Bolan nodded.

"And me?"

Nancy Rhynman's eyes bored into Bolan's. "You require further study," she said.

"Well enjoy. Meanwhile I'm going to go chat up the boss," Bolan said as she walked away.

Eckhart had laid his rifle down and he and Rai

were discussing some salient point about Kalashnikovs. Rai looked up at Bolan inscrutably through his hooded eyes. He suddenly beamed and patted the AK-103. "Good kit."

"Thanks." Bolan nodded to Eckhart. "The rest of the men seem to approve as well."

"I approve, too, Coop," Eckhart said. "My buddy said you were solid. Piet thinks so, too, and his word is gold with me."

Bolan knew where this was going. "But?"

"But I can't find out jack shit about you, and believe me, I've tried. Then again, my buddy kind of implied you don't work for Uncle Sam."

"I don't work for Uncle Sam." Bolan went with the truth but not the whole truth. "We've had what you might call a working relationship in the past."

Eckhart grunted in amusement. "Well that's some spooky-ass shit."

Bolan nodded. "I've been spooky."

"Okay, but if you don't work for Uncle Sam—" Eckhart put on his boardroom face "—why the hell are you here?"

Bolan gave Eckhart a hard smile. "Because a very good friend of mine, someone I trust, someone I owe favors, said your brain is a national treasure. One we can't afford to have splattered across some godforsaken rock in the corner of Tajikistan, and could I please help keep it in your cranium. I said yes."

"Well, shit, Coop!" Eckhart suddenly beamed. "Sexy talk like that'll get you a date to the prom!"

Bolan changed the subject. "Tell me, are you and Nancy an item?"

Eckhart gazed down the firing line as Rhynman stood and filled out her fuzzy pink sweater. "God, I wish."

BOLIN LAY on the bed in his guest cottage and compared notes with Kurtzman.

"This could be the real deal. We've been running every angle and raiding the national archives of every nation who could have any clue on this, and there is a chance that Eckhart is on to something. I can understand why he's going under the radar. He wants the patrimony of being the man who finds it. This could be the biggest archaeological discovery in a century," Kurtzman said.

"Interesting, but why do the Chinese care?"

"Well that's the weird thing. From your jump-off point into the mountains it would take months to ride into any territory that's claimed by China. Why they're so excited about this is a serious unknown."

"Bear, I have an assassination attempt in Atascadero and now an abduction attempt in London. Eckhart seems to be just a man who's giddy about an archaeological discovery. If he has another agenda then he's fooled all of us including me."

"He is a self-made billionaire. They're tricky people."

"I've spent time with the man. I've felt his vibe, and until proven otherwise I'm saying his action is legit. Something else is going on here. What do we have on our prisoner from the Atascadero hit?"

"Nada," Kurtzman said. "The FBI still has him and he hasn't uttered a word."

"What about the woman at the Stafford?" Bolan asked.

"Same situation. MI6 has grilled her and she hasn't so much as asked to use the bathroom. All they know is her ID says she's an immigrant from Yugoslavia and it's fake. Beyond that she's a ghost."

"Bear, give me something. Anything. Work me up a situation."

Kurtzman took a deep breath and let it out. "I only have one thing on my mind at the moment, but it's going to complicate things."

Bolan had long ago learned to trust the hunches of Aaron Kurtzman, no matter how badly they complicated his life. "What's that?"

"You had a full-on guns blazing and damn the collateral damage in Atascadero."

Bolan had already seen the contradiction. "And London was a clear-cut kidnapping attempt," he said.

"Striker, my gut says we have more than one player in this situation."

As usual, Kurtzman had confirmed Bolan's worst suspicions. "Assume one is the Chinese," he said.

"Right, and since you're headed to Tajikistan, which just happens to be a former Soviet republic, let's assume the other is the Russians," Kurtzman concluded.

"That's the way I see it," Bolan agreed. "And the Russians and the Chinese wouldn't risk an international incident to kill or kidnap a billionaire over a possible archeological dig."

"I see it that way, too."

"So find me something, anything," the Executioner said. "No matter how far-fetched it seems."

"You got it."

"You have the files I sent you?" Bolan asked.

"I do. The men all check out. That's quite a band of jolly pirates you've joined there."

"Any anomalies?"

"The only real question mark is Yuli Simutenkov. We don't know what he did for France. The French Foreign Legion files don't have too much about him."

"Anything else?"

"Evo Waqa was indeed part of the mutiny by the Fijian counterrevolutionary unit. However, he's distantly related to Fijian royalty, so rather than prison or dishonorable discharge he was given KP duty for a year. Apparently he thrived on it and now he's quite the chef. Rumor is he wants his own cooking show when he's done with soldiering."

Bolan shrugged. "So we'll eat well."

Kurtzman laughed.

Bolan was only half-joking. Soldiers marched on their stomachs and they were going to be pony trekking for weeks through the roughest mountains in Central Asia. What Evo Waqa could do with their rations was going to be intensely important in everyone's life. "I'll feed you any information as available, but I have a feeling once we're in-country Eckhart is going to insist we go dark." Bolan checked his watch. It was time to go.

6

Dushanbe, Tajikistan

Dushanbe was a city that had grown according to no particular plan. Old-world Asian architecture clashed with Soviet-era block buildings. Modern hotels, shopping centers and office buildings had popped up in the city center and were slowly spreading outward. Tajikistan had declared its independence as the Soviet Union fell apart and like a lot of the former Soviet republics it had fallen into a devastating civil war. For a little over a decade things had remained fairly peaceful but it still remained the poorest country in Central Asia. Heroin flowed across the sieve-like border with Afghanistan. The Russian Mafia and the local clan-based Tajik gangs fought bitterly for control of the drug trade when they weren't cooperating. Drug money had brought corruption into the highest levels of government. The kidnapping trade was endemic. Government opposition groups were slowly sliding into Islamicterrorist movements and outside the major cities things got wild, wooly and tribal very fast.

Despite all this Tajikistan was considered a beacon of light in the region. They had welcomed international assistance and made great strides to re-integrate former civil war combatants. The elected government was friendly to both the east and the west, and had allowed Russia, France and the United States to station troops within her borders for various security missions.

A little money in the right place could smooth out any situation. Fake IDs and travel documents had been procured with ease. Smuggling in the guns and gear had been even easier. Eckhart was posing under a false name as a potential investor in the country's booming ecotourism industry. His little army of mercenaries were posing as fellow investors and international consultants.

Tajiks were falling over backward to assist them.

They had arrived at Dushanbe Airport and been led to a private cargo area where the team armed and armored up. Their suits had been tailored to accept soft-body armor. Bolan wore his Stetchkin machine pistol in a shoulder rig, the snub-nosed R-92 on his ankle and a Czech Mikov switchblade rode in his back pocket. The rest of the team tucked away Makarov automatics and their personal choices in tactical blades. A trio of Mercedes limousines was waiting for them outside the baggage area as were the remaining members of the team.

Professor Bartholomew Penn was a little gnome of a man. He was balding, bespectacled and decked out in ill-fitting khaki safari clothes that looked ridiculous on him. He greeted each man with a firm handshake. Penn had brought a small team of graduate students with him to help with the dig if it happened. Stewart Steeves was a mini-Penn right down to his receding hairline, spectacles and wardrobe. However he did not share his mentor's respect for soldiers. He couldn't keep the disdain off of his face as he met the security team.

Tim Beakman was from South Central L.A. His hair, mustache and beard were all of the same length and prematurely graying. He was older than the average grad student but he'd had to work to put himself through school. Part of that work had been as a combat engineer with the Army National Guard to earn the Montgomery G.I. Bill. He hadn't seen combat but he had worked several natural disasters, including Hurricane Katrina, and according to Eckhart had participated in several successful Mayan archaeological expeditions in Mexico. If they found an archaeological site he would be the dig master.

Stina Swartz looked like a goth girl with an eating disorder who had gotten lost on the way to a rave and ended up in Tajikistan. She had stopped just short of facial piercings but her pageboy hair was dyed black, her clothes were black and her skin was vampire pale. However, Bolan noted her hiking boots were brown and well broken-in and Eckhart whispered that her knowledge of all things Alexander was encyclopedic and her IQ was higher than the entire team's put together except maybe for Nancy's.

Team Endeavor piled into the limos and headed for downtown Dushanbe.

Nearly all the cars on the street were Russian Ladas with a sprinkling of equally boxy-looking Skodas and Yugos. The occasional BMW, Mercedes or Russian Zil luxury sedan were evidence of the money pouring into the Central Asian nation. Bolan was in the lead limo with Eckhart, Nancy, Rai, Professor Penn and his grad-student shadow Steeves. He continually scanned the traffic around them. "Where're we headed?"

Eckhart responded. "Hotel Mercury. It's not the Stafford but it's comfortable and we aren't staying long. I'm arranging helicopters to take us and all our equipment to our jump-off point. I have a connection here in Dushanbe who knows a horse trader he swears by. He's due to meet us with a herd for us to choose and some men who are supposedly trustworthy."

"How many locals?" Bolan asked.

"One guide and he's bringing along four clansmen to maintain the horses, help with the grunt work and deal with any locals we encounter on our trek."

Bolan's eyes slid to a four-car convoy of Lada sedans. Each of them had cheaply applied purple tinting film concealing the interiors and a custo-mized fabric covered sunroof. Bolan's hand moved to the grips of his machine pistol.

Rai cleared leather and flicked off his pistol's safety. "What?"

Eckhart looked back and forth between them. Nancy sucked in a breath. Professor Penn looked excited and Steeves swore.

Bolan drew his Stetchkin and pushed off the safety. "Something, maybe nothing." Bolan took out his tactical radio and clicked it on the open channel. "This is Coop. We've got four cars coming up on the left."

Blackpool responded from the second limo. "Bloody hell."

Piet answered from the third limo in the caravan. "Eyes on, Coop."

"Get all noncombatants down on the floor, now. Be ready to—" Bolan snarled as the four cars all lunged forward and the car roofs were ripped back. "Here we go!" Bolan pushed the selector of the Stetchkin to full auto and punched the button on the limo's sunroof.

The enemy was a step ahead. A man in the lead Lada rose up. He was wearing dark glasses and a yellow bandana was pulled over his face. He had a large shotgun aimed at the lead Mercedes. Bolan rose up in the limo's sunroof and shoved his machine pistol out in a two-handed hold. The giant shotgun boomed. The Executioner squeezed off a burst from the Stetchkin and the gunner's head misted red as it was hit by a swarm of lead.

But the damage was done. The hood of the Mercedes flew up and smoke and steam erupted as the shotgun round impacted. The limo driver stood on his brakes like a fool and Bolan nearly flew out into traffic. The limo behind rear-ended them and the third followed—exactly how the enemy had planned it. They'd been hit with a Russian 23 mm round consisting of a solid steel slug the size of a wine cork. The round had been designed to crack an engine block. The limo's motor screamed and clanked and Bolan knew they weren't going anywhere.

He fired the rest of his magazine into the sedan as it passed and its rear window cratered like the moon.

The tinted windows of the other three sedans rolled down and stubby barreled automatic rifles protruded.

Bolan slammed a fresh magazine into his pistol and vainly wished they had their rifles and support weapons. Team Endeavor members rolled down their windows and prepared to do battle but when it came to weight of shot they were going to get the worst of it. Bolan reached his left hand down into the limo. "Eckhart! Give me your gun!" Bolan roared.

Eckhart slapped the pistol into the big American's hand.

Bolan leaped from the limo. The sedans slowed as

they began their firing pass and the vehicles ex-changed their broadsides. The carbines buzz-sawed in the assassins' hands. Team Endeavor fired back but their pistols were underpowered and loaded with hollow-point bullets to compensate. They were never intended to penetrate cars. The killers' carbines had no such problem and tore through the limos as if they were tin cans. Bolan could hear Nancy and Stina screaming.

He had one advantage. Cars were difficult to fight out of. Only the men in the sunroofs were able to maneuver their weapons with any ease. The sedans had slowed to deliver their full magazines into the stalled limos and Bolan ran straight at the lead car. The driver was pointing and screaming at him. The man in the sunroof turned just in time to take a burst in the face. The men in the car tried to bring their carbines around in the narrow confines of the sedan but Bolan had already jumped up on the hood. The men within screamed and died as the Executioner fired burst after burst down through the sunroof.

Bolan dropped the spent machine pistol and jumped onto the road. The shooter in the second sunroof shuddered as ZJ and Yuli put him in a cross-fire and his carbine clattered to the street. The driver was shouting and grinding gears. His window went opaque with blood as Bolan pulled the trigger of Eckhart's weapon. Bolan flung open the door and shot the Lada's other three occupants. He tossed the smoking, empty Makarov, picked up the fallen carbine and shoved the selector to semi-auto.

The tail car of the drive-by had seen enough and its tires screamed and smoked as it shot in reverse. Following Bolan's lead the members of Team Endeavor had left their vehicles and swarmed around the fleeing car. It crashed as the driver and other occupants died in a hail of bullets.

The men were charging the final Lada in a wedge formation and firing as they closed in.

Bolan dropped the empty rifle and ripped the little snub-nosed revolver from his ankle holster. Up ahead the lead Lada was stopped. Two cars had gotten into an accident as they had rushed into traffic to get away from the firefight. People behind them had abandoned their vehicles and fled leaving the intersection a snarl of stalled vehicles. Bolan charged forward. The door of the lead limo flew open as Rai joined him. Rai fired his pistol as fast as he could pull the trigger. Bolan reserved his own ammo.

The driver of the Lada panicked. He shot his car into Reverse and turned himself sideways; he was attempting to plow his way up onto the sidewalk but he was snagged atop an abandoned motorcycle that someone had dropped. His tires were squealing and rubber was burning but the motorcycle was jammed against his front axle and slowing his progress to a crawl. Bolan and Rai approached. The Gurkha threw down his empty pistol and drew his khukri from its sheath. The driver had made the further mistake of presenting the driver's side of the car to his pursuers. The backseat shooter was desperately unrolling his window. He shoved his carbine out clumsily with one hand like a giant pistol.

The war cry of the Gurkha ripped out of Rai's throat. His khukri flashed and the carbine and the hand holding it fell away ribboning blood to the pavement. Rai ignored the screaming assassin and drew back his weapon for the driver. The driver yanked his gearshift, stomped on his pedals and keened like an animal caught in a snare. Rai slung his massive blade forward. It sank into the driver's skull.

The two remaining gunners were hampered by confines of the sedan and the dead man who had fallen back through the sunroof. Bolan climbed onto the trunk of the Lada. He fired into the interior until the men were down. The surviving assassin collapsed into his seat clutching his arm.

Bolan reached into the Lada for a new rifle. "Rai, I'm going to check on the others. You got this?"

Rai slammed his khukri back in its sheath, picked up a fallen carbine and checked the loads with a nod. "I have this. Check on the others."

Bolan ran back to the convoy. He could hear Stina screaming for a medic. In limo number two Blackpool was on the floor in a sea of his own blood. His face was fish-white with blood loss and shock.

Stina had stripped off her black sweatshirt and folded it into a compress. Her pale skin crawled with tattoos. Her arms were covered with blood as she applied compression to the wound. She gave Bolan a wild look. "He needs a medic! He needs a medic now!"

The Endeavor men were rifling the corpses for IDs and intel. Bolan shouted, "Gilad! Man down! Medic!"

The Israeli commando came at the run. He crawled into the limo and knelt beside Blackpool. He pulled aside the soaked compress and his face went grim. "Cooper! We need medivac! We need it now! We need—"

Blackpool's last breath came out of his body like a bellows squeezed until the handles met. He bled out and died.

Bolan clicked his radio. "Team Endeavor, sound off!"

The team came back across the radio. Those within sight of Bolan waved. Bolan saw blood running down Yagi's left arm but he signaled to say he was fine. Eckhart spoke across the radio and his voice shook. "Cooper, we have a casualty."

Just about every man there was a veteran and it had been assumed from the start that Piet was the military leader, but it was very clear that Bolan was in command at the moment. "Giddy, with me." They raced to the lead limo. Nancy was crying. Eckhart was clearly in shock. Professor Penn held his graduate student's bloody head in his lap. Gilad shook his head. A bullet had pierced Stewart Steeves's skull. The limo driver's head was flopped to one side. His cap and the top of his head were gone.

"Giddy, Rai has a prisoner up front. I want you and Yuli to do some field intelligence," Bolan said.

Gilad shouted over his shoulder as he ran toward Rai. "Yuli! With me!"

Bolan went back to Eckhart. The billionaire had been very cavalier about attempts on his life, but now he had lost team members and there was genuine shock and loss on his face. The Executioner stuck his head into the blood-drenched limo as sirens wailed in the distance. "Sir, with a little money in the right places this will be chalked up to a kidnapping attempt, but we need to get our story straight and then get out of town ASAP. Your enemies know you're here." Bolan leaned in close enough so that only Eckhart could hear. "And when you have a spare moment, you and I need to talk."

7

Mack Bolan stood in the barn before a folding table loaded down with evidence. The team had extracted from the road battle in town to a farmhouse near the foot of the mountains. It was a small meeting. Eckhart, Piet, Rai and Bolan stood around the table as wind and rain pattered on the corrugated roof. Yuli and Gilad were the other two attendees. Bolan got straight to business. He picked up one of the commandeered carbines. "This is a *Vikr* or Whirlwind compact assault rifle." Bolan held up a bullet he had taken from the magazine. The round was short and thick, but the most striking thing about it was the black needle tip of tungsten steel that stuck out of the copper jacket. "This is an SP-6 armor piercing round. That's what chewed up the limos." Bolan put the weapon down and tapped the giant shotgun. "You know what that is, Phil?"

"The biggest goddamn shotgun I've ever seen?" Eckhart tried.

"That's right. You're a hunter. You've fired a twelve gauge?"

"Yeah."

"A ten gauge?" Bolan prompted.

"Oh yeah." Eckhart nodded. "They kick like mules."

"Well that right there is a four gauge. The call it a KS-23 because the Russians took rejected 23 mm aircraft cannon barrels and turned them into shot-guns. They were designed with two things in mind. Stopping riots and stopping automobiles."

Eckhart stared at the brutal weapon.

Yuli lit a cigarette and blew smoke toward the rafters. "*Da,* what Cooper says is correct."

"That wasn't just a drive-by, it was a professional hit. At least as professional as money can buy in Taji-kistan. If they'd had RPGs we'd all be dead and now that we're out of the city we should count on it," Bolan said.

Yuli nodded. "This is also true."

Everyone quietly contemplated being hit by rocket power. Eckhart sighed. "Well, shit, Coop. What's the good news?"

Bolan looked to Gilad. "You get anything out of Lefty?"

It was a bad joke but everyone laughed grimly. Gilad shrugged. "Not too much. The police were coming. Time was short and I had to tourniquet his arm, but the people who hit us were Uzbek gang-sters."

"Uzbeks are biggest minority in Tajikistan. Much of heroin that comes through Tajikistan continues north through Uzbekistan. Always turf war between Tajik and Uzbek gangs in capital. Uzbek gangs well known for ruthlessness in holding and defending territory," Yuli said.

"Do we know who hired them?" Bolan asked.

"The guy said it was a pair of Russians and they paid in Euros." Gilad scratched at his sparse beard. "From what I could get out of him they sounded like cut-outs."

Bolan kept his thoughts about the Chinese and the Russians to himself for the moment. "Anything else?"

"Not really," Gilad said. "I could have worked him harder, but I don't think he really knew anything more. He's just a shooter. Someone else was pulling the strings."

Piet shook his head. "So, all we know is that someone unknown wants to kidnap or kill our employer."

Eckhart scowled. "Yeah, apparently. Anyone got any more good news?"

Piet sighed. "Much will depend on whether the enemy knows what we're doing and where we're going. In our favor—" Piet smiled wryly "—even we don't know exactly where we're going or what we are doing. It will make us unpredictable."

Eckhart failed to see the humor and gave the South African a sour look. Gilad glanced out toward the rain-shrouded peaks in the distance. "Maybe we can shake them in the mountains."

Rai spoke for the first time. "We are a big party. Tomorrow we take on local guides and porters. Call our numbers at least twenty. Two horses per man, plus pack horses for equipment and gear. That many men, that many horses? Hiding our tracks will be very difficult, and it has just rained."

Eckhart was still waiting for some good news. "So what do we do if we can't shake them?"

"We take them down," Bolan's eyes went steely. "Yuli, ZJ, Blair and I all have mountain fighting experience, and the rest are all combat veterans. That's why you hired us. And frankly, once we're up in the mountains we shouldn't wait around on our enemies. I say we go proactive on these guys."

"Da!" Yuli apparently liked what he was hearing. "Cooper is correct! Take battle to enemy. Defensive fight in mountains is last, worst option."

Eckhart looked to Piet. The South African veteran's pale eyes were focused on the middle distance and seemed to be reviewing some very hard-fought battles. "I have no experience in mountain fighting like this. I did most of my fighting in the jungles and on the veldt. However, the strategy of warfare is still the same. Waiting for the enemy to attack you is never good. Best to be proactive as Cooper says. We make the mountains ours, become the hunters rather than the hunted."

Eckhart's gaze flicked from man to man. What had started off as an adventure to find lost ruins was starting to sound like all-out war. His eyes fell on Piet again, as if the South African was his anchor. "Okay…so how do we do that?"

Piet turned and spent long moments considering the mountains ahead of them. "I am sniper-qualified. Cooper, I saw you zeroing in one of the Dragunovs. I assume you have some sniper training as well?"

It was something of an understatement. "Yeah," he said simply.

"Good." Piet had made his decision. "Sniper-scout teams, then. Yuli was born in the mountains. He and I will take lead and range ahead to probe for ambushes. Cooper will take the rear team. He will range behind us, shadowing our tracks and see who comes following us."

Bolan approved. For a group of people wandering around Central Asia like lost sheep with assassins on their trail it was the soundest strategy.

Piet raised an eyebrow at Bolan. "Coop, who do you want on your team?"

"I'll take Blair. I don't like him but he did a lot of fighting in Afghanistan. He'll understand the mission as well as anybody."

"Good, very good." Piet looked to his employer. "Mr. Eckhart?"

Eckhart seemed to gain resolve now that there was a plan of action and the die was cast. "Okay, Piet. You'll brief the rest of the team tomorrow before the helicopters come to pick us up. Before we get airborne collect everyone's cell phone and issue tactical radios. Anything else?"

Bolan nodded. "We lost Blackpool. We're down a man. According to the file you showed me Tim Beakman was in the National Guard. I want to issue him a rifle."

Eckhart frowned. "Well, he was an engineer and was never in a war zone, but he must have qualified with a rifle in basic. Yeah, give him a gun if he'll take it. Anything else?"

"Yeah." Bolan nodded at the massive KS-23. "Make sure we pack that."

THE RUSSIAN MI-8 HELICOPTER swept over the Pamir Mountains. Waqa was the hero of the morning. He had raided the henhouse and whipped up a hearty breakfast. The sheep farm employed dozens of men during the shearing season and the kitchen was equipped with several giant, Turkish copper coffee-pots. By the time he was done Team Endeavor had started the morning well fed and with the best cup of coffee any of them had had in recent memory. His place in everyone's heart had been secured when he stole one of the *ibriks,* the coffee mill and a ten-pound sack of coffee beans.

Eckhart left money to pay for it.

Stina Swartz was heaving her breakfast into a paper bag. The rain had stopped but the winds over the mountains were ugly and the helicopter leaped and bucked. A few stage-whispered jokes flew around the cabin behind her back but she was beyond caring. There was no point asking her if she was all right. She wouldn't be until they landed.

Bolan put a hand on her shoulder. "We're almost there."

She whimpered and resumed her heaving.

The archaeologists were all sitting together as a unit so Bolan crouched beside Tim Beakman. "Word is back in the day you were a combat engineer," he said.

The archaeologist stared at Bolan noncommittally. "Back in the day? Yeah, man, that was indeed true."

"So you know how to shoot."

"Oh, I qualified with an M-16, but barely. Marksmanship wasn't my specialty and shooting people sure as shit wasn't why I joined the Guard." Beakman rolled his eyes. "I took that G.I. ride to get my degree. I was an engineer, but first and foremost I'm an archaeologist. I haven't lifted a weapon since basic." Beakman looked Bolan up and down in open suspicion. "And I think you're asking me to go commando on this thing."

Bolan gave Beakman the straight deal. "We lost Viv. People want us dead. I'm not telling you, but I'm asking. We have a couple of spare rifles. I want to give you a one-day, AK intensive and issue you a weapon."

Beakman considered the unexpected and unwanted development. Then he smiled. "Fuck it. I'm down.

And if there's one thing I do know how to do that's how to launch a grenade like a motherfucker. I should've been quarterback."

Bolan nodded. "We'll talk later."

As Bolan rose Nancy Rhynman put a hand on his arm. She leaned in close and whispered over the hammering of the massive rotors over their heads. "I want a pistol, and I want you to show me how to use it."

Bolan didn't throw her words about not believing in guns back in her face. He spoke quietly. "You sure?"

"I don't know how much help I can be if we're attacked, but I don't want to be helpless." The hand on Bolan's arm was shaking slightly, and not just with the vibration of the helicopter. "I don't ever want to be helpless like that again."

Bolan nodded. "The first day we make camp and have a spare hour I'll set you up."

The helicopter began to circle down out of the sky and the pilot's voice came across the intercom. Yuli shouted out a translation. "We land! Secure seat belts!"

Bolan watched the earth spiral beneath them. They were landing in a valley like a knife cut between two mountains. A small village clung to one side of the foothills like a beehive of clay cubes and grain fields covered the hillsides heavy, golden and ready for harvest. What held Bolan's interest was a corral the size of a soccer field swirling with scores of horses that were mostly gray, bay and chestnut in color. The thunder of the helicopters had gotten them riled up and some raced around the enclosure while other jostled and reared.

The chopper landed on the moist ground. Yuli slammed open the cabin door and men laughed as Stina desperately flung herself out. Bolan checked the loads in his AK, deployed the folded stock and slung his weapon. The rest of the soldiers followed suit. They formed a loose phalanx around Eckhart and the noncombatants as they disembarked. A group of locals came out to meet them. The oldest was clearly the leader. He walked with a stick and was draped in the traditional shawl, scarf and woolen cap that was common all over Central Asia. He smiled to reveal his missing front teeth. The other five men wore jeans and boots, but up top they wore heavy sheepskin jackets and were swaddled in wool shawls and caps. Each man carried what looked like an oversized chef's knife on his belt and a lariat loosely in his right hand. Two of the young men were twins who were still in their teens and the last one looked barely old enough to ride. Bolan suspected looks were deceiving.

Eckhart had hired some Tajikistan cowboys.

Yuli made the introductions and nods, smiles and pleasing gestures were made all around. "Head man's name is Hamid," Yuli said. "He welcomes you to the village and looks forward to a good day of horse trading. He wishes to know if you will take tea?"

Eckhart grinned and nodded at the old man. "Tell him I would be honored."

8

They rode deep into the mountains. ZJ had instantly won everyone's respect as a horseman. He also spoke some Russian and the cowboy from Budapest got along famously with the Tajik wranglers. He spent a lot of time riding up and down the line making sure everyone's tack, harness and horses were working out. He spent even more time riding beside Nancy Rhynman and seeing to her every comfort on the trail.

Blair, on the other hand, was clearly the worst rider on the team. He was going to be saddle sore in the morning. He spent his time muttering about the hired help and making cruel jokes they couldn't understand.

The men he had insulted continued to watch over him and his painful progress solicitously.

Bolan knew he'd be sore as well. The team had ridden hard the first day and were making camp in a little canyon while it was still light. Waqa leaped from his horse, built a fire and started brewing coffee. By silent unanimous consent he was excused of all fatigue duties for the rest of the trip.

Setting up tents, digging the latrine and hobbling the horses was accomplished with speed and precision.

Eckhart smiled slyly. "Well, we should probably save the champagne for when we find the Citadel, but…"

All heads turned as Eckhart walked over to one of the packhorses and untied a crate wrapped in a tarp. "Since this is the first official day of our endeavor—" he heaved a case of beer out of the packing and pressed it over his head "—I think a little celebration is in order!"

The soldiers whooped. Eckhart went over to the little stream beside the camp and nestled the cans into the frigid waters. "Should be cold by the time dinner's ready, boys!"

Cheers rang throughout the camp. It wasn't much but a cold beer was an unexpected perk on the trail and would cut the dust of a hard day's ride.

Bolan turned as Beakman and Nancy approached. Beakman had a rifle slung over his shoulder and he saluted smartly. "Corporal Beakman, reporting for duty."

Nancy smiled with uncharacteristic nervousness and saluted. "Nancy Rhynman, girl in need of a gun."

"Mr. Eckhart," Bolan called. "I need a few beer cans for target practice."

Blair pointed a finger at Bolan in outrage. "Oh, you suck, Cooper!"

Bolan requisitioned three beers and he, Nancy and Beakman walked into a side canyon sipping beer. "Let's get to it," he said.

The Executioner ran through the differences between the M-16 and the Kalashnikov. Beakman was an engineer and just short of being a college professor. Loading, reloading and the manual of arms he grasped instantly. Bolan placed the three empty cans on a boulder at the end of the canyon and walked back to the imaginary firing line.

Beakman peered through his optic, closed his eyes and yanked the trigger. His bullet impacted just short of the lip of the canyon wall. Beakman went on to put twenty-nine more rounds into the dirt of the canyon floor, the walls above and every rock and shrub in between. The beer cans seemed to have invisible halos over them. Nancy suppressed a smirk. "I told you, man. I can launch a grenade like a—"

"You don't get a grenade launcher until you knock down one of those cans," Bolan said. "That's a forward-mounted, low-power optic on that weapon. I want you to keep both eyes open."

Beakman considered this. "Okay …"

"And keep your eyes open when you pull the trigger. No one likes a flincher. Then, before every shot, I want you to take a long, easy breath." Bolan opened his hand and slowly made a loose fist.

"Then let half of it out. Caress that trigger. Don't pull it. Take up the slack so slow the shot is a surprise."

"Okay." Beakman internalized the information, put in a fresh magazine and shouldered his weapon.

"No pressure," Bolan said.

Beakman laughed, but it made him relax and he consciously took a long breath. His face contorted as he forcibly fought his habit of flinching and kept both eyes open.

Bolan spoke very quietly. "Whenever you're ready. Take the shot."

Beakman peered through his optic. Breath quietly hissed from his mouth as he let half his air out. Very slowly the pad of his forefinger pushed back and took up slack on the trigger. The AK-103 suddenly cracked. A beer can flew into the air.

"Yeah!" Beakman roared. "Oh, hell yeah!"

"Steady down, do it again."

It took him seven more shots but he sent the remaining two cans flying across the canyon. Nancy clapped. "Give the man a cigar!"

"I'm going to give the man a grenade launcher actually. God help us." Bolan nodded in approval. "Slow fire. Chew those cans up. Then pick a tree branch or a rock. I want you to fire five more magazines."

Beakman was eager to shoot. "Right!" He resumed firing.

Nancy stared at Bolan with mixed emotions. "My turn?"

The Executioner reached into his pocket and pulled out the Russian snub-nose. "This is a revolver."

"Six-shooter," she said, nodding.

"Five-shooter actually." Bolan broke open the action. "This is the cylinder. Five holes, five bullets, its about as simple as a gun gets." Bolan ejected the five-round ammo cassette and put it back in. "That's all there is to it." He thrust out the little pistol in both hands. "Shooting hand pushes, off hand pulls. Put the front sight on your target and squeeze." Bolan put the front sight on the trunk of a fallen tree about seven yards away and pulled the trigger five times. Five holes appeared in the wood in a pattern that could be covered with a coffee cup. "You try."

Nancy took the pistol and a spare cassette of ammo gingerly but managed to open the action, eject and reload without too much fumbling. She held the pistol out in both hands and squeezed the trigger. She made a little yip as the gun went off but wood flew.

Bolan nodded. "Again."

She fired four more times. Three of her bullets hit the trunk and one was a flyer. Her hands shook a little as she lowered the pistol and looked at Bolan. Hitting a tree at seven yards wasn't exactly tack-driving, but Bolan noted with approval that save for the little start on the first shot she wasn't a flincher, and despite being a first timer she had counted her shots and not pulled the trigger a sixth time. Bolan handed her a box of ammo. "Reload, do it again."

DAWN ROSE CLEAR and cold over the Pamirs. Waqa was already up brewing coffee and simmering a huge pot of buckwheat kasha in broth he'd made from last night's goat bones while everyone else began striking camp. Bolan found Eckhart and Professor Penn huddled over a map. It was a photocopy of an ancient piece of leather. Eckhart had exhausted every available piece of technology to enhance the map and fill in the missing pieces. The two men hunched over the map protectively as Bolan walked past. Piet had collected the team's cell phones and each member had been issued a tactical radio. The party had a pair of sophisticated laptops with satellite links, but only Yagi, Eckhart and Rai had the access codes.

No one was calling out without permission.

Blair groaned. "Fuck!"

Bolan watched as the ex-Ranger hobbled bow-legged to a large rock and eased himself onto it. He shoved his pants down to his knees and shook his head in disgust.

Blair's legs were well muscled but his inner thighs looked like hamburger. He was going to come up lame if something wasn't done. Piet looked over and frowned at the abrasions. "Gilad! Medic!"

Two Tajik horsemen approached smiling and

nodding. One held a dripping plastic bag. He reached in and took out two goat steaks that had been chilling in the icy creek overnight. He pointed at Blair's saddle sores and handed over the steaks. Blair applied them directly where it hurt. The ex-Ranger's eyes nearly rolled back in his head with relief. He grinned up at the two Tajiks. "You two are fine little helpers," he said.

The men nodded again and smiled happily.

BOLAN AND BLAIR ate and deployed. Blair had re-applied his meat packs with some bandages from a field dressing and he was already riding taller in the saddle. They rode silently along their route and took up an observation post Bolan had noted in a cleft of rocks overlooking the trail.

The Executioner's eyes went to slits as he scanned through his binoculars. "What do you make of that?"

"What?" Blair peered through his own optics at a gully two miles away. "That's a big fucking dog."

The dog was mastiff-size, probably running something between eighty and a hundred pounds. It was shaggy and its cropped ears were cupped against its head like seashells. It was joined by a second and they were sniffing along the trail left by the horses. Men on foot appeared behind the dogs. They were carrying rifles and occasionally stopped and knelt.

"Fuck," Blair said.

Bolan clicked on his tactical. "Piet, this is Coop. Blair and I have contacts two miles back, definitely tracking us, definitely armed."

"Acknowledged, Coop," the South African said. "Be advised, Yuli and I have detected armed contacts ahead."

9

They were pinned. The dogs and trackers came on behind them. Men on horseback soon followed. All of them had guns. Bolan, Blair, Gilad and one of the Tajiks watched them from behind cover a little less than a mile away. Bolan clicked his tactical. "Piet, what have you got up front?"

"Armed men, platoon strength," Piet said. "The Tajiks believe the men ahead of us are the retainers of a very bad man named Shukrat."

"How bad is bad?" Bolan asked.

"Apparently most heroin comes up from Afghanistan, but the Tajiks have a few regional producers of their own," Piet responded. "This man Shukrat is one of them, and a man of evil reputation. Though, according to Yuli, the Tajiks are surprised to see them here."

"They're operating outside their territory," Bolan said.

"Yes," Piet confirmed. "What have you been able to ascertain?"

Bolan glanced at Gilad. "Anything?"

Gilad and their guide spoke in whispered Russian. Gilad shook his head. "He says he doesn't know who these guys are. He says despite their clothes they are not Tajiks."

Bolan locked eyes with the guide and shook his head. "Not Shukrat?"

The man understood and shook his head unhappily as he answered in Russian. *"Nyet."*

Gilad didn't look happy, either. "He says he is concerned because these men behind us can only have come from the direction of his village."

Bolan surveyed their trackers and didn't blame him. "Piet, how are the guys ahead of us armed?"

"Well…" Piet was quiet for a moment as he scanned things on his end. "They're opium soldiers in Central Asia, Coop. It's a hodgepodge, but it's all Russian kit."

A thin smile crossed Bolan's face. "Blair, what do you make of those rifles down there?"

"I don't know." Blair shrugged as he gazed into his binoculars. "I think they're all carrying Russian AKs."

"No." It was a subtle difference but Bolan's life often hinged on such things. "They're all carrying Chinese Type 81s."

Blair did the math. "Fuck."

Bolan nodded and clicked his radio. "Eckhart, you there?"

"I copy, Coop."

"I think the people in front and behind are two different groups. I'm thinking it's possible they don't even know about each other. I think the people behind us are Chinese. If the group ahead of us belong to this Shukrat character, someone has got them motivated to range outside their area."

Eckhart wasn't panicking yet but he was clearly agitated. "What are you saying, Coop?"

"I need more intel, but my first guess is that the people behind us don't know where we're headed and are following us. Up ahead, someone else knows exactly where we're going, and they put this Shukrat in our way."

"Coop?" Eckhart's voice rose slightly. "*We* don't know exactly where we're going."

"Yeah," Bolan replied. "Kind of funny, isn't it?"

Blair shook his head as the trackers inched closer. "Coop?"

"Yeah?"

"You're freaking me out."

"So?"

Blair lowered his optics and gave a grin. "So maybe we should we go down there and fuck with those guys."

It wasn't the worst idea Bolan had ever heard. "You know something, Blair? You're okay."

"Yeah, well." Blair shrugged. "You know."

"But I have a better idea."

"I was hoping you'd say that. What's on your mind?" Blair asked.

"We've got shooters in front of us and shooters

behind. Now I could be wrong, but I think these groups have two different agendas." Bolan lowered his binoculars and saw the ex-Ranger's grin. "I say we introduce these guys and watch what happens."

"HERE'S HOW IT GOES." The Executioner scratched a map in the dirt with the tip of his bayonet. He had assumed command again. Neither Piet nor Eckhart said anything, and no one else objected. "We're going to use these guys."

Eckhart and his archaeologists looked nervous.

"You have a plan?" Piet asked.

"The guys behind us could have caught up already if they pushed hard. They're not interested in taking us, at least not yet. They want to see where we go." Bolan pointed his stick into the map ahead of them. "I think someone else entirely put these guys in our way. Piet, what's their disposition?"

"As you say, Coop. They await us in ambush. I do not believe they are professional soldiers. The only support weapons I saw were RPGs. All the rest of their weapons were Russian small arms. I saw little in the way of optics or sophisticated equipment."

Bolan nodded. "I want to rile up the guys ahead of us then draw them right into the guys behind us."

Piet frowned at the scratches in the dirt. "A neat trick."

"These guys are used to feuding and pushing peasants around. If they take any real casualties they'll melt away. I want a short clash and then we fake a panicked retreat. With luck they'll go into wolf-pack mode and try to run us down," Bolan said. He looked to Yagi. "What did you get us?"

"I believe I have our bolt-hole." Yagi produced a satellite map. "This entire area is a series of canyons. The map Mr. Eckhart and Professor Penn are using is a copy of a map that is over two thousand years old. This area of Central Asia has been subject to violent seismic upheaval. Glaciers have melted and reformed. Rivers have changed their courses." He tapped a series of squiggles making a C-shaped course. "This is a series of canyons. We passed the entrance to the first one half a mile back and it is little more than a cleft in the rock. If we go from here, to here, to here, this will lead us to a valley and from there back to our projected path. According to the latest satellite imaging all of these canyons are currently open. However, it will be at least a forty-eight-hour detour. The weather is inclement and these canyons are subject to flash flooding. I must also warn you that some of the terrain will be difficult for the horses."

Bolan set the plan. "ZJ, you need to ride right now and set a series of charges across that opening. Blair, go with him. We'll be coming fast and bringing company. We may need counterfire before ZJ blows the charges."

ZJ and Blair ran to get their gear. Bolan turned to the rest of the team. "Yuli is keeping an eye on the guys ahead, so we're going to see them before they see us. I want our civilian elements well back. Yagi, Waqa, Beakman. You're up front with me. When we make contact I want you guys to shoot a lot and not hit much." Bolan shook his head. "Beakman, that shouldn't be a problem for you."

Beakman rolled his eyes while the rest of the men laughed. "Asshole."

Bolan tapped the map of the ground ahead of them. "I want these guys surprised then I want them to see us scatter like bunnies. Got it?"

The team all nodded.

Piet scratched the white stubble on his chin. "And what about our six?"

Bolan tapped his dirt scratchings. "That's where you come in. Once the team is in retreat I want you to take out a couple of the guys behind. Not just the trackers, they're probably locals. I want one of the guys on horseback. I want them to know the jig is up. One or two and then extract. We fall back into the canyon, ZJ closes the door behind us and we let our playmates sort things out between themselves."

"Timing will be everything," Piet said. "But not a bad plan. Better than getting pounded between the hammer and the anvil."

Bolan rose and sheathed his bayonet. "Let's move."

BOLAN RODE POINT with Waqa, Yagi and Beakman. He'd swapped his sniper rifle for an AK with a grenade launcher. Yuli's voice came across the tactical. "When you come around the bend enemy will have visual."

"Copy that. Tell me when they see us." The bend was only thirty yards away. "You heard him, look sloppy, stay sharp." The horse was tense beneath Bolan. She wasn't skittish or shying but she sensed her rider's intensity and matched it. She was like an arrow laid across a bow and waiting to be released.

They came around the bend. Yuli instantly radioed in. "They see you! They are bringing weapons to bear!"

Bolan vocalized into his mike. "Closest?"

"Eleven o'clock!" Yuli responded. "There is a cleft in the rock face!"

Bolan roared, "Look out!" He couldn't see the concealed men but he shouldered his rifle and sparks and stone chips flew as he burned a magazine into the position. He shouted loud enough to wake the dead. "Back! Back! Back!"

"Five o'clock!" Yuli shouted across the line. "Three!"

Yagi and Waqa began firing. Bolan reared and wheeled. "Back! Back! Back!"

The Executioner and the forward fire team galloped back the way they had come. Behind them voices shouted in a mix of Tajik, Russian and Arabic and automatic weapons sprayed. The voices were exultant, pointing out targets and shouting commands. Horses spilled into the ravine and the warlord's riders thundered in pursuit.

Bolan spoke into his tactical. "Yuli, extract!" He risked a look back and saw all of his team was with him as they rounded the bend and were momentarily out of harm's way. Bolan spurred his horse and she shot ahead of the pack toward Eckhart and the rest of the team. Bolan pointed his rifle back over their heads. "Ride!"

The men wheeled and raced for the tiny gap behind them.

Bolan gave Piet the signal. "Do it!"

"Acknowledged!" Bolan could hear the South African's semiautomatic sniper rifle begin cracking in his earpiece.

Bolan turned his horse and shoved a fresh magazine into his rifle. His men stretched into single file and charged through the knife slash in the rocks. Yuli came into view riding for his life. "They come!" he shouted. "They come!"

He charged into the cleft as Bolan flicked up the ladder sight on his grenade launcher. He squeezed the trigger and the rifle bucked against him as it launched its 30 mm payload high into Yuli's pursuers.

ZJ appeared in the narrow confines of the cleft and waved his detonator. "Coop! Come on!"

Bolan did a mental head count and came up one short. He shouted across the tactical. "Piet!"

Bolan snarled. "Piet! Respond!"

"My horse is down! It's all shite! Go, Coop! Go now!" Piet was breathless and running and bullets cracked in the background.

The horse reared as Bolan pulled on the reins. "ZJ! Anyone comes through the gap besides Piet or me—blow it!"

Zoltan shouted in consternation. "Cooper!"

Bolan shouted into tactical. "Piet!"

Piet shouted back. "I'm pinned down!"

"Run!"

"What?"

"Run!" Bolan commanded. His horse pounded down the path. Piet suddenly came into view. His limbs churned woodenly in an exhausted lumbering run. He caught sight of Bolan and tossed his rifle. His fists pumped as he redoubled his efforts. Bullets cracked into the rock wall behind him from enemies Bolan couldn't see yet. He leaned out of the saddle and thrust out his arm. He and Piet's hands slammed wrist-to-wrist in the mountain climber's handshake and Piet violently left the ground.

The big American grimaced with effort. Bolan heard the South African's shoulder pop and dislocate. Piet's grip loosened but Bolan held on, using momentum to swing the man around and behind him. The horse whinnied as she took Piet's weight and Bolan pulled on the reins to turn her. Bolan saw horsemen spurring toward them on the path ahead. Bolan shouted over his shoulder, "Piet! Start shooting!"

Piet clawed awkwardly for his pistol left-handed. Bolan spurred the horse on but she had lost her momentum. Her charge was spent and she had just taken on a second passenger. The little mare could carry both men until end of the world but she couldn't run beneath them. She tried anyway. Her legs stretched out and her hooves dug into the ground in a laboring echo of her former sprint.

Bolan's radio crackled. Gunfire snapped and popped in strange stereo as the sound of shooting echoed off the rock walls and in his earpiece. Waqa was shouting over the sound of gunfire. "Coop!"

There was a firefight going on at the gap.

"Now!" the big Fijian shouted. The unmistakable sound of an RPG rocket detonating shook the canyons. Waqa shouted desperately. "Now or not at all!"

"Inbound!" Bolan roared back. Piet's pistol began returning fire behind them as they rode. A terrible sound of effort groaned out of the over-loaded little mare's heaving lungs as she lowered her head and dashed for the gap.

A battle burst into view. Waqa and Yagi guarded either side of the gap and were laying down suppressing fire. Blair knelt behind a boulder a little past them and the PKM machine gun rattled off bursts. Down the path dozens of men were firing back from behind rocks or the bodies of their horses. Beakman stepped out of the gap, fired his grenade launcher and stepped back.

A bullet cracked past Bolan's ear as the enemy

behind closed in. Piet fired his pistol dry and couldn't reload one-handed. Yuli and Gilad stepped out of the gap and it almost seemed they were shooting right at Bolan as they engaged his pursuers.

The horse threw back her head and screamed as she was hit.

The little mare stumbled and nearly spilled her riders. She fought to keep her feet. She screamed again in agony and effort as she regained a semblance of control and righted herself. She plunged through the gap with her legs failing. Her hooves churned the soft sand of the cleft for another thirty yards and then her knees buckled. Bolan kicked out of the stirrups and cleared his horse as they fell. He hit the sand hard but managed to roll with the blow and came up on his feet and his pistol cleared leather.

Waqa, Beakman, Yagi and Gilad ran past. Blair kept shooting until the last moment and was twenty yards behind. He ran clutching his machine gun to him like a man running out of a burning building holding a baby. "Now! Now! Now!" he shouted.

Riders appeared in the gap.

Bolan whirled and chopped his hand at ZJ. "Do it!"

The little Hungarian pumped his detonators and the gap exploded. Blair was knocked to the ground as rocks funneled down the narrow ravine and washed over the team in a wave. Bolan ran forward and heaved Blair to his feet by his web-gear. The ex-Ranger yawned and blinked against the blast but training took over and he automatically began running down the ravine. Bolan waited and listened. Settling rock cracked and sand sifted. The dust and smoke began to clear enough to see that the gap was gone. In its place was a rock slide of impressive proportions.

The stunned silence outside suddenly erupted with gunfire from the direction of the drug lord's men. It was instantly answered and the other side of the blocked pass turned into Armageddon.

Bolan wheeled around. They had to cover some distance and do it fast. One of the Tajik wranglers approached him with a fresh horse. The young man gazed up at Bolan in open hero worship. There was simply no greater act of bravery than to fly back into the face of the enemy to retrieve a fallen comrade. Bolan nodded and took the reins.

10

They rode hard and the weather held. They were ahead of schedule and over halfway through the maze of canyons Yagi had chosen as their route. They were keeping cold camps but had encountered no more enemy patrols.

The Executioner rode up beside Eckhart and Piet. Gilad had popped Piet's arm back into its socket but it still had to be immobilized in a sling. The South African sniper wouldn't be doing any precision marksmanship anytime soon. Bolan had given Piet his machine pistol to compensate and Piet carried the Stetchkin on his hip as well as a Makarov in a cross-draw holster. Piet was chewing painkillers dry as Bolan rode up. "How's it hanging, Piet?"

Piet winced as he lifted his shoulder slightly. "Feels like it's hanging by bloody threads, but it beats a shallow grave in this land of sand and rock, I'll tell you." He toasted Bolan with the little amber pill bottle Gilad had issued him. "I owe you my life."

"Don't worry about it, we need to…" Bolan's voice trailed off as he looked over at Rai. He was staring fixedly up into the northern sky. He saw nothing up in the gray vault over the Pamirs. "Rai?"

"Planes, Cooper." The Gurkha made a face. "Fast movers."

Bolan raised his binoculars. The planes were coming head on and so fast it was difficult to keep them in the binoculars' field of view. They were dark gray, shaped like spearheads and had no visible markings. The Executioner had an ugly suspicion they had come from the Russian Air Force's Special Purpose Command. The unmarked Fencer pair were coming in very low and very fast. Their wings slid out like shark fins as they slowed and aligned themselves with the canyon Team Endeavor was traversing.

Eckhart's head ping-ponged between Bolan and Rai. "What the—"

"Incoming!" Bolan roared. "Scatter! Move! Move! Move!"

The scream of the Fencers' engines warbled and howled as they flared their flaps and dropped even lower to start their attack run.

Eckhart stared in panic as his team galloped in every direction possible all around him. "What's happening?"

"We're about to get lit up!" Bolan slapped the flanks of Eckhart's horse. The horse reared and nearly spilled its rider before shooting down a side ravine. The scream of the jets filled the sky. The

Fencers were expecting no countermeasures or meaningful ground fire so they were descending to do their work up close and personal. Fire strobed beneath their bellies and their automatic cannons made a sound like God tearing the world in half. Humans and horses screamed as they were torn apart. Bolan knew the gun run was just the appetizer.

Nancy fought her rearing horse. "Cooper!"

Bolan seized the reins of her horse and rode down the side ravine after Eckhart. The jets flashed past and out of the corner of his eye Bolan saw the canisters beneath their wings release.

"The river!" Bolan shouted. Heads turned but there was no time to explain. He could only lead by example. He reined back and Nancy screamed as Bolan tackled her out of the saddle and the two of them plunged into the river.

The cold was like a fist to the jaw.

The turbulent gray surface closed over them and they hit bottom. The riverbed had been carved from solid rock and was as wide and deep as a grave. Rocks battered them as they tumbled blindly. Bolan managed to seize one. He pulled Nancy's thrashing body tight against him and hugged bottom. The world above went orange as the thermobaric weapons detonated.

In the U.S. military they were called fuel-air explosives. The Russians called them vacuum bombs, but the effect was the same. At a designated height the proximity fuse dispersed a cloud of liquid explosive charge and a second charge instantly ignited it and propagated a blast wave. Pound for pound they were far more powerful than a conventional high-explosive bomb but their effects were far more unpredictable.

Nancy went limp in Bolan's arms. He waited several seconds for another blast but when none was forthcoming he spent long moments fighting his way to the surface. The swift running river had pulled them farther along than he had imagined. Bolan's limbs and face burned with cold as he clawed his way onto the riverbank.

Bolan's lungs sucked raggedly at the air and instantly filled with the burning tang of explosive residue. He hacked and coughed and pushed himself to his knees. There was no time to rest. Nancy's eyes rolled in her head as she choked and gagged. He rolled her onto her side and she coughed up the river water she'd swallowed. The Executioner stood shakily. It would be useless if the fighter jets returned but his numb fingers instinctively curled around his pistol. Clouds of black smoke and dust rose into the sky. The rock walls of the ravine almost seemed to glow. Their orange and red colors were all the more brilliant from having been scrubbed clean by the searing pressure wave.

Bolan yawned at the ringing in his ears and walked to his horse. The animal had come out from around an elbow in the ravine about a hundred yards back. It felt like a mile as Bolan walked it. The stocky mare stood singed and shuddering but at first glance seemed to be all right. She shied slightly but steadied under Bolan's hand and let him lead her.

He slid his rifle from its scabbard and swiftly checked it over.

Nancy rose swaying to her feet looking pale and shell-shocked. Eckhart and some others were pulling themselves out of the river. Blair and Yuli had been on point and were far enough away from the blast that they appeared to be unscathed as they rode in. Bolan put Nancy on the horse and then began walking back toward the epicenter of the blast.

Someone had just risked war to make sure Team Endeavor never left the mountains alive.

11

The Team Endeavor had been hammered. The cold, tactical part of Bolan knew it could have been far worse. Fuel-air weapons were most famous for their use in Afghanistan as bunker busters and collapsers of caves and tunnel complexes. The maze of canyons and ravines had given the unpredictable weapon all sorts of avenues to explore and much of their power had vented up into the sky.

But it had been bad enough.

Team Endeavor was busy digging graves. Three of the Tajik cowboys were wrapped in blankets. The others clasped their shaking fists together and rocked and wept over their kinsman's bodies. There wasn't much left of Stina Swartz but Bolan zipped a scorched sleeping bag closed around what remained. Waqa had slept in two bags zipped together because of his size and girth but it only took one to make his death shroud. Bolan zipped the bag closed. No hardship had phased the big man from the South Pacific. He had kept his good humor throughout and under combat conditions had taken gristle and bone and turned it into a banquet. Bolan had been depending on the big Fijian to keep the team's spirits up when things got bad.

Gilad sat on a rock with a dazed look on his face. As team medic he had wanted to help but Bolan had forced him to rest. When the Executioner held up a finger and asked the Israeli how many he'd blinked and earnestly answered "Three." Gilad had a concussion. Nothing was leaking out of his ears or eyes but it was a bad one.

ZJ's eyebrows were gone, his perfectly manicured mustache and Vandyke beard had been charred down to stubble and his face was a bright baby-pink from flash-burns but he stood in a pit with his shirt off, shovel in hand on grave detail. Rai had been burned much worse. One side of his head was wrapped in bloody bandages and one look had told Bolan the Gurkha's left eye was gone. His left hand had been damaged as well and it was wrapped mummylike in oozing bandages. Eckhart, Piet, Penn and Beakman had all managed to hurl themselves into the river. Eckhart and Beakman seemed ashamed that they had escaped unscathed. The rocky ride tumbling down the river hadn't done Piet's shoulder any favors. Professor Penn's boot was the only thing keeping his ankle from inflating like a football. Bolan would have to probe it later to see if anything was broken and splint it. Yuli was bruised from being thrown by his horse.

Roy Blair was looking as blond, tanned and fit as

Captain America out of costume and seemed utterly unrepentant about it.

Bolan considered their supplies. The good news was they were in Pamir Mountains in fall so water was everywhere. The bad news they were up in the Pamir Mountains in fall and at night the temperature dropped precipitously. They had lost most of their propane and many of the tents were blackened wads of plastic. Many of the plastic packed MREs were badly seared and might not be edible.

Only six functioning tactical radios survived and they had been locked on a closed channel. The spares and extra batteries had been blown sky-high with the horses that were carrying them. The collected cell phones were gone and like a lot of the tactical radios the ones that hadn't been rounded up had gone swimming in mountain streams. The spare satellite link was gone. Yagi squatted over the remaining one, muttering Japanese invectives when he wasn't coughing. He had been close to the epicenter, closer than some of the dead, but due to the capriciousness of fuel-air weapons he'd somehow managed to avoid incineration. He had breathed in superheated air and fuel-air explosive fuel. He could function but the air up in the mountains was wet and cold, and he couldn't stop coughing. If they didn't get down out of the Pamirs soon and get him to a doctor infection would set in, his lungs would fill and Gobun Yagi would drown in his own juices.

Bolan walked over. "Yagi, what have we got?"

"It's messed up, Coop. I don't know if I can fix it with what I have on hand. I only have one spare battery and the charger is toast," he said, coughing.

Bolan nodded. "Keep trying."

The worst thing about the situation was the horses. Three-quarters of the animals had been killed or so badly injured they had to be put down. Half of those that remained were shell-shocked, suffering from burns and marginal rides at best.

Bolan walked over to Eckhart. The billionaire had taken a turn digging and his palms were blistered and raw. He sat on a rock and watched the soldiers dig graves with a sick look on his face. Piet was gray-faced with pain and exhaustion. Bolan put a hand on Eckhart's shoulder. "Mr. Eckhart."

It was a full three seconds before Eckhart started and looked up at Bolan.

"Sir, you're the leader of Team Endeavor. As soon as we get the bodies in the ground I need you to say a few words over them." Bolan looked up. The sun was starting to set and rain was starting to mist. "Then we're going to have a meeting. Not just you, me and Piet, but everybody." Bolan took a long breath and let it out. Things were going to get a lot worse before they got better. "Anything and everything is everybody's business now."

"I'M TAKING COMMAND." The Executioner said it quietly and matter-of-factly. No one objected. Most of what was left of Team Endeavor was hunching against the sleeting rain in their ponchos and most seemed not so secretly relieved that someone was taking ownership.

ZJ spoke up. "Those were Russian fighters." He gave Yuli an ugly look. "Who would have called them in?"

Yuli gave the little Hungarian a contemptuous shrug. "Russians would have called in, but do not look at me, little man. I am deserter from Russian army. I joined Foreign Legion and swore fealty to nation of France. Russian army will shoot me given opportunity."

Blair spat. "A guy who turns traitor once will do it again. In fact I hear it gets easier each time."

"Like all Americans." Yuli rose to his feet. "You talk too much."

Blair stood to meet him. The two men suddenly found Bolan between them. "I think everyone needs to shut up while I'm talking," he said icily.

Yuli and Blair glared but they didn't make a move. Tensions were riding high. Bolan decided that the facts of life might focus the survivors. "First we need food. Yuli, tell the cowboys to pick the most likely horse carcasses and butcher and salt as much meat as we can carry. We've got a long walk ahead of us."

Like a lot of Russians of his generation, Yuli understood what missing a meal meant. He turned a blind eye to Blair and began relaying orders. The two Tajiks nodded, grimly drew their knives and wandered out into the rain.

"Yagi," Bolan continued, "we need extraction. What have you got?"

Yagi shook his head at the satellite rig on his knees. "Stuff is broken inside and something is wrong with the antenna interface. We definitely can't send, but if I shake it around sometimes I pick up some signals. Faint and distorted."

"Keep working on it. I have friends looking for me and so will our employer." That brought Bolan to the matter at hand. "Mr. Eckhart?"

The billionaire lifted his face up into the rain. "Yeah, Coop?"

"We got nuked."

Eckhart lowered his head again. "I don't know why."

"Sure he does." Blair's handsome face was an ugly mask dripping rain in the gloom. "I say we beat it out of him. Fuck his thousand dollars a day."

Rai gave Blair a very weary look with his remaining eye and before anyone could blink his pistol was in his hand, resting on his knee and vaguely pointed at Blair. "I have taken a contract. I will see it through," he said.

Gilad had been in a glazed stupor for the last hour but now he raised his hand. Bolan nodded at him. "Giddy?"

"Not to overstate the obvious but one of us works for them."

The group grew very quiet as what everyone was thinking came out in the open.

Piet rose with an effort. "It does not matter. Our communications are smashed. Only survival matters now. I am with Cooper."

Bolan smiled wearily. "You don't know what I'm going to say."

"I know exactly what you will say," the South African said. "Enemies before us, enemies behind us and fighters in the sky. We will never walk back to Dushanbe, or even to a village. Someone wants to stop us. It seems others follow to see where we will go. I believe completing the mission is our only option. If we achieve our objective perhaps we have a bargaining position. Meantime? Perhaps we get our communications working and call for extraction." Despite his utter exhaustion an ugly light came into the man's pale eyes. "Or we kill our enemies and take theirs. Either way I say forward. Back is only death."

"Piet's right." Bolan shrugged. "That's what I was going to say." A few desultory laughs met the statement, but the survivors were desperate for a direction, and even more desperate for a ray of hope. "Anyone who wants to try it on their own is welcome to leave, and you can take as much horse meat and ammo as you can carry, but the horses stay with the team. And if you're going to do it—you do it now. After that anyone who tries a breakout or steals the team's supplies will be executed."

Bolan looked from face to face as he spoke. "Right now, show of hands. Who's in?" Everyone raised their hand, but in the depths of Bolan's heart he knew Gilad was right.

There was a traitor among them.

12

Bolan awoke to the sound of rotors and rolled to his feet. Dust sifted from the roof of the cave with the vibration. The group had wandered lost for two days before stumbling into a cave that had clearly been used by travelers for centuries.

The cave was spacious. Someone in antiquity had taken the time to level the floor. Holes in the wall were regularly spaced and had obviously once held sconces for lanterns or torches. Along the far wall was a slightly lower sandy space. In several places long troughs had been carved into the rock. Bolan guessed there was enough room for a dozen horses to rest comfortably. Central to the cave was a fire pit. The spit or tripod was gone, and there was little in the way of furnishings. Ancient travelers, particularly important ones, would have brought their own camp cots, rugs and tapestries to hang from the walls. The one exception was a clay box about the size of two refrigerators laid on their backs. There was a blackened hole in one side of the box to feed embers from the fire. Bolan had seen smaller versions of such things in China. Millions of Chinese, particularly in the north, slept on such beds. The interiors were literally clay ovens that kept the sleeper warm on the coldest nights. Bolan had never seen a king-size version of such a bed before.

The group was so exhausted they immediately took shelter and everyone slept.

The Executioner picked up his AK and shoved a 30 mm anti-armor round down the muzzle and clicked it in place. ZJ stuck his head through the blankets covering the cave entrance and sunshine flooded the area. "We have company!"

Soldiers leaped to their feet. Civilians sat up in confusion. Bolan stepped out of the cave to find ZJ and Yuli grimly surveying the sky. A giant helicopter hammered the air over the mountains as it orbited over the tortured rock formations.

The Executioner had been on the wrong end of Mi-24 Hind gunships more times than he cared to think about. They were the heaviest armed, armored and fastest helicopters in the world. This particular Hind was more disturbing than the average. It was painted a matte, nonreflective black and had far too many antennas and sensors sticking out of the fuselage for Bolan's liking. The cabin doors were open and men wearing heavy body armor leaned out over their heavy machine guns. Spotters with optics stood next to them scanning the mountains.

Yuli crushed out his cigarette. "*Spetsnaz,*" he said.

Having failed to fireball Team Endeavor out of existence it seemed the Russians had sent their best of the best to do it up close and personal. Bolan called back over his shoulder. "Beakman! ZJ! Grenade up! Antiarmor!" Bolan nodded at Yuli. "Break out the RPG. Get everyone geared up for a fight."

Yuli raised an eyebrow. "You mean to take the gunship down?"

"I want to bring it down before it sets down and deploys men. When they can't find us from the air they'll deploy scouts. Once they have us pinned down in the cave another vacuum bomb will incinerate what's left of us. We can't ride out of here until we clear the sky."

Yuli ran back into the cave without another word. Team Endeavor had packed a RPG-7D that broke down into its component halves for airborne troops. Blair came out snapping a grenade into his launcher and deploying his folding stock. "Hey, Coop."

"Yeah?"

"Won't the Ruskies be expecting this?"

"No." Bolan shook his head. "They wouldn't be flying this low if they knew we had support weapons."

Blair gave Bolan a hard look. "So why didn't the asshole among us tell them?"

"Because he works for the Chinese, Blair." Bolan flipped up the grenade launching sight on his rifle. "And the Chinese want that Russian chopper down as bad as we do."

Blair's broad shoulders sagged. "Oh," he said quietly.

Yuli came out with an assembled and loaded RPG-7D. One of the guides followed him carrying three spare rockets. The rest of the team came out armed and assembled beneath the overhang. Bolan glanced upward as the rotor noises thundered louder and the Hind approached again in its orbit. "Those of you with rifles—they won't do much against a Hind—so shoot into the open cabin doors. Even better let's get a few hits with grenades. You all have optics. Use them. Shoot for the smoking holes and see if you can help rip things up a little more."

They waited until they could feel the concussion of the rotors slapping the sky directly overhead.

"Grenadiers," Bolan said and stepped out from the overhang into the open. "Now!"

The Executioner put his sight on the point where the helicopter's fuselage met the tail boom and fired. His round smashed into the boom a yard away from where he had planned but smoke and fire blossomed and the chopper jerked. Beakman, Blair and ZJ's 30 mms all thudded and the armor-piercing rounds delivered their shaped charges and shot molten fire into the chopper's tail. The plan was simple. Without its tail rotor the Hind would lose control and fall.

The problem was the Russian nickname for the Hind was "flying tank."

The helicopter swung around and dipped its nose to bring its cannons to bear on its assailant's. Bolan felt the heat of the backwash against his neck and shoulders as Yuli sent a rocket-propelled grenade into the chopper. The bird shuddered and continued its spin. Bolan slapped another grenade into the muzzle of his 30 mm and fired at the bulge of the starboard engine housing. The grenade spiraled away and his finger curled around the trigger of his rifle. He put the aiming circle of his optic into the open cabin door and held the trigger down on full auto. Blair, Beakman and ZJ's second salvo hit the chopper in the cheek, chin and spine. But the grenade launchers fired too slowly and their trajectory was too looping to get the kill shot on the moving helicopter. Sparks whined across the entire length of the helicopter as Eckhart, Rai, Yagi and Gilad emptied their weapons into the airborne behemoth.

Bolan slapped in a fresh grenade and a fresh magazine as the helicopter stabilized. The AK slammed against his shoulder as he lobbed his grenade for the pilot's canopy but the munition spiraled high and hit the air intakes. Blair, Beakman and ZJ got another three grenades on target but the airborne tank lived up to its name and steadied itself in the sky. Bolan aimed his rifle at the blackened mess of the air intakes and burned another magazine into the wreckage.

The Hind's door-gunner drew a bead on Team Endeavor and his PKM sent a stream of tracers down into the ravine. Gilad was stitched from skull to scrotum with armor-piercing rounds. Yuli sent another rocket screaming into the sky, and smoke and fire exploded around the tail boom. The Executioner slammed in his last antiarmor round, took an extra second to aim as the door-gunner traversed onto him and pulled the trigger. The grenade spun upward and the pilot's cockpit filled with orange fire. The chopper spun as the incinerated pilot lost hold of the stick. The door gunner's burst went high and wide and only his chicken straps kept him from being hurled into space. The starboard observer next to him wasn't so lucky and as the chopper tipped he screamed as his gloved hands slipped on the door frame and he plunged to his doom into the rock maze below. For a second the chopper was helpless in the sky. "Yuli!" Bolan roared. "Finish it!"

Yuli took aim and the third rocket sizzled upward. The chopper suddenly and quite deliberately slewed sideways across the sky. Bolan grimaced and the Russian swore a blue streak as the rocket missed. The weapon sailed past the tail of the besieged chopper and detonated hundreds of yards up in the sky like a giant bottle rocket.

The Hind had two cockpits and the weapons operator had remedial stick and rudder controls. The weapons officer had taken the stick. Blair, Beakman and Zoltan put another three grenades into the chopper's sides as the weapon's operator dipped the nose of the smoking Hind to bring his cannons to bear. Blair screamed as he fired. "We're out of armor rounds!"

"Anything!" Bolan shouted. He aimed his rifle and put another thirty rounds into the gaping hole in the air intakes he'd created. "Bring it down!"

The Hind's walls had been breached but the siege was far from over. An engine screamed and clanked but the Hind had two of them. Bolan slapped in a fresh magazine and fired on full auto. He watched his rounds spark off the armor glass cockpit. Frags slammed against the sides of the chopper and one detonated in the troop compartment but it wasn't enough. The twin barreled 30 mm cannon spun on line to point at Bolan.

"Yuli!" Bolan shouted.

Yuli was swearing at his launch tube. Something was wrong.

Even Bolan was surprised at the streak of yellow fire and smoke that suddenly screamed across the valley and flew straight into the flame flickering around the Hind's tail. The ant-aircraft missile detonated and the beleaguered tail boom of the Hind separated like limb falling from a tree. The main fuselage spun out of control. The main rotors snapped off as they hit the rock formations and the body of the chopper fell sixty feet and screamed and buckled as it scraped against the walls of the ravine. The fuselage dipped and the chopper hit the ravine floor nose-first like a lawn dart. Smoke and flame shot skyward as the ruptured fuel tanks blew. Cannon shells and munitions began cooking off in strings.

Blair reloaded and watched the chopper burn. "Jesus…"

Beakman lowered his smoking AK with shaking hands. "I could be wrong, but, uhhh…I think we're going to have to score that one an assist."

Bolan reloaded. "Yeah." He turned to Gilad's body. "ZJ, Blair, put him in his bag. We'll bury him at our next stop. Someplace where the wolves won't dig him up." He walked back into the cave. Professor Penn was the only member of the team who hadn't participated in the fight but he'd never fired a gun in his life and he had torn ligaments in his ankle.

He looked up hopefully as Bolan entered. "Did we win?"

"Yeah, sort of. Listen, how are we doing on a direction?"

Penn warmed to the idea of being useful. "I think we're on the right track. This part of Central Asia is earthquake country. Over the course of two thousand years the Maze, as our guides call this area, has changed. That's why we kept hitting dead ends, but when we found this ravine I think we found the straight shot to the finish I remember from the map. We've mostly crossed the Maze."

"Do you really think you can find this Citadel?"

Penn nodded. "I think so. Yagi's memory is pretty much photographic but he was following a map where the lay of the land had changed. Now we have a direction and I suspect he remembers the rest of the map as well."

"Okay." The Executioner walked back out. He shook his head at the vast black plume of smoke rising into the sky from the murdered helicopter like a road sign. "Everyone saddle up. We need to ride far and we need to ride fast."

13

The door to the Citadel was closed. Team Endeavor
had pushed hard. They made no effort to conceal
their tracks. All they cared about was making
distance between themselves and their pursuers and
reaching their objective. They had left the Maze
and ridden two to a horse to cross a flat plateau.
They knew the burning wreck of the Hind would
draw their pursuers in and after that it was a race and
Team Endeavor was hobbled. In their favor Yagi remembered the map perfectly and what had been
confused and contradictory before now suddenly
made sense. They descended into canyon country
again and in the late afternoon they had found it.
Much like the way station, it was cave beneath an
overhang of rock. Only this cave was closed. Indeed
it appeared to be sealed. Bolan wasn't a combat
engineer but the door appeared to be made out of
concrete. Fortunately Team Endeavor happened to
have a combat engineer with them.

Beakman sighed at the sealed opening. "Not like

this is going to be an epiphany for anyone, but yeah, that's poured concrete, and very distinctly less than two thousand years old." He nudged his horse forward and pointed at the seams. "Definitely poured from the outside rather than in. Someone locked this place up tight and without much regard for getting back in."

Bolan nodded at their demolition man. "ZJ, get us in there."

The little Hungarian grinned and reached behind his saddle for his bag of tricks. Professor Penn waved his arms frantically. "You're going to blow your way in? God only knows what you might damage! That's the archaeological discovery of the century in there and …" Penn's voice died at the look in Bolan's eyes.

"Professor, that's concrete. Someone's already discovered it," Bolan said. "The Russians have already tried to nuke us. Then they sent in gunships. You want to wait around in the open and see what they try next?"

"Yes. I mean, no. I …" Penn stuttered.

Bolan sighed in fatigued tolerance. "ZJ?"

The Hungarian was busy sorting through his detonators. "Yes, Coop?"

"Try to limit the behind-the-wall aftereffects."

The demolition man drew himself up in offended dignity. "But of course! Take pry-bars, I need a series of small holes around the edges." ZJ described an eight-point arc around the sealed entrance. "There, there, there. You see?"

Team Endeavor had abandoned all but one pack-horse load of tools. Bolan drew a digging bar from the weary packhorse's load. "Piet, go back a mile. Get on the escarpment and let us know if anyone is coming. Blair, Beakman, Yuli, you're with me."

Piet rode out while Bolan and his wrecking crew got to work. It was not a large job but it was laborious to drill into concrete with hand tools. It took far longer than Bolan had hoped. The sun was sinking fast as they finished the last hole. The big American wiped sweat from his brow and stepped back. "ZJ, blow it."

ZJ began placing charges of plastic explosive into the holes. He pulled out his detonator box and grinned. "Fire in the hole!"

Little geysers of smoke and dust erupted in an arc around the barrier. The Hungarian sighed with satisfaction.

Eckhart stared at the wall that still stood before them. "Now what?"

ZJ stared in disbelief. "You chop in, find some rebar, tie a rope around it and use the horses to pull it down."

That job went quickly and within fifteen minutes men and horses were straining at the ropes.

"Here it comes!" ZJ shouted.

The concrete wall fell like a drawbridge with its chains cut. Team Endeavor coughed at the cloud of dust and cement particulate. Bolan checked the loads in his rifle, clicked on the tactical light attached to it and stepped inside.

Eckhart pushed past him. "What do you see? What do you…my God."

Alexander the Great's Citadel of Hades was indeed a "house of weeping columns with walls of glittering stone." The way station had been a snug pocket in the earth. The Citadel was a vast subterranean vault where stalagmites as thick as redwoods rose to meet stalactites and form giant wasp-waisted columns. Formations of quartz and crystal studded the walls, floor and ceiling like diamonds and threw off millions of glittering reflections from the flashlight beams. Someone had carved a winding path through the vast hall that was wide enough for two horses to ride abreast. Team Endeavor entered the fairy-tale-like cavern and even the most jaded amongst them were awed.

"Fuck me." Blair stared about in wonder. "This is it, isn't it?"

Nancy led Professor Penn's horse. The old academic looked to be very quietly ready to burst into flames. "Yes, Mr. Blair. This is it," she said.

Part of the main vault had been cleared to form a sort of stable. The ground had been leveled and smaller stalagmites had bronze rings set in them for hitching horses and other niches for lamps or torches. Water trickled from a cleft into a long stone trough carved into the wall of the cave. Bolan's finger never strayed far from his trigger. Something was wrong, he could feel it.

The Tajiks began seeing to the horses. Bolan

looked back the way they had come. "ZJ, you and Yagi go set some charges at the door, antipersonnel, and then keep an eye out. Blair?"

"Yeah?"

"Carry the professor."

"What? Why me?" Still grumbling, the ex-Ranger slung Penn piggyback. Penn was grinning. He'd been afraid he was going to be left with the horses and gear as usual. At the back of the vault they found a maze of chambers. Some were natural caves and others carved in the rock. Stone oven beds, basins and carved couches of stone demarcated living areas. Others were simply empty spaces designed for storage. One room contained a cistern. Penn noted different carving techniques from room to room and it was clear that the Citadel had been added to and modified over time by different occupiers. Past the cistern they found a carved staircase that wound upward almost vertically through the rock.

At its foot they found a body.

Most of the team recoiled at the sight of it. Bolan and Yuli dropped to their heels beside it. Yuli scowled and lit a cigarette. "He die badly."

The man had died very badly. He wore a nondescript blue coverall, work boots and an empty tool belt. The air inside most parts of the cavern complex was bone-dry and so was the corpse. It was an excellent environment for natural mummification. Bolan had seen such corpses before and his brows knitted. Air-cured humans turned into a sort of beef jerky. This man's corpse swam in his clothes like a stick figure. What little meat there was on his bones was vacuumed against them. The skin of his face and exposed hands was pitted like Swiss cheese. Yuli crossed himself. "Rats have been at him."

Bolan shook his head. He'd seen corpses with the same markings before only much fresher. "No, he had smallpox."

Most of Team Endeavor lurched back in alarm.

Bolan glanced up the pitch-black spiral of the staircase. "He was infected and he was starving to death. I think he got too weak and fell down the stairs." Bolan turned back to the team. "His own people sealed him in to contain the infection."

"Smallpox?" Blair scoffed. "I had that when I was a kid."

Nancy Rhynman turned on the ex-Ranger. "Blair? If you were any dumber you'd have to be bigger."

"What?" Blair looked around the team.

Professor Penn spoke quietly. "You're thinking of chicken pox, Mr. Blair. This man had smallpox. It's estimated to have killed three hundred to five hundred million people in the twentieth century alone. Smallpox is believed to be the greatest killer of humans in history. People worry about Ebola and other viruses, but smallpox is a proven quantity, Mr. Blair, the big kill. If this man died of starvation or falling down the stairs then he was lucky."

"Shit!" Blair took a step back. "Is he contagious?"

"I doubt it," the Executioner said. Several team members gasped as Bolan reached toward the corpse and snapped off a pair of dog tags. He gazed at the Cyrillic script and handed it to Yuli. The Russian held them up into the light of his tactical.

"Timofei Vadim, private, combat engineer, Far Eastern Military Dis-trict. Most likely he was involved in sealing of Citadel."

Blair was still backing up. "Yeah, until he got his ass infected and his buddies buried him alive in here. I say we bug out and take our chances outside."

Bolan shrugged. "Go ahead, but leave the professor here."

Bolan began climbing. The stairs were so steep they almost qualified as a ladder. Iron chains had been set in the wall but they had rusted down to their mounting rings. He came to the top and found himself in a passage he had to stoop to fit through. He could hear Blair swearing and squeezing his bulk up the stairs after him followed by the others. He followed the passage for a few dozen yards until it ended at an ancient wooden door bound in bronze. It opened reluctantly with a squealing of hinges. Another king-size stone bed dominated the room. A pair of chairs with a table between them had been carved right out of the rock. The open door to an antechamber gaped to one side. The walls were covered with carvings and inlays. Penn reached out his hand from his perch on Blair's back and ran a hand over a carving. "Most of the works below were clearly Persian. The work in here is Greek."

Blair set the professor in one of the chairs. "So, the master bedroom?"

"Most likely," Eckhart said.

Large clay jars were lined up against one wall. Two of them had been opened and the stench of rancid oil and spoiled vinegar filled the room. Bolan walked across the room. A natural, four-foot chevron shape in the rock wall had been filled in with concrete. Bolan consulted his mental map. The passage doubled back over the main cavern. "This room overlooked the ravine," he said.

Penn clapped. "Yes, and it faces east! It would have let in natural light during the day, and fresh air." Penn smiled as he looked around. "A luxury in a cave dwelling, even one as luxurious as this." He frowned at cracks in the ceiling and the walls. "There's been earthquake damage. Some of it recent."

Nancy knelt beside one of the giant jars. Blair wrinkled his nose at the smell. "I don't think the Russian found anything worth eating in there."

Nancy ran her hand over the jar. "Most of it has flaked off but this one was painted. This one was for something other than oil or wine, but the Russians didn't recognize it."

Blair drew his knife. "Let's bust it open."

Penn exploded. "No! We need to get a team in here with equipment. We need—"

"Yo, Prof." Blair curled his wrist and exposed his watch meaningfully. "The Russians are coming. The Chinese are coming. You want to see what's in there? Now's the time."

Bolan had to concede it might have been the brightest thing Blair had said during the entire expedition. "Mr. Eckhart? Nancy?"

Phillip Eckhart was glowing and Nancy Rhynman was close to jumping up and down and clapping her hands. Eckhart nodded. "Do it. Carefully."

Blair methodically began cracking the clay seal around the top of the jar. After a minute he got the lid moving. He recoiled at the stench as the lid came off. "Goddamn!"

Nancy had rolled up her sleeves and reached boldly into the jar with both hands. She turned her head away and her nose wrinkled. "Ick!" She came up with a dripping, viscous prize and by the shape Bolan already suspected what it was. Nancy brought out the dripping package. "Oil is an excellent preservative, particularly if you can seal it away from air," she said as she began unwrapping blackened and beslimed cloth away from the two-foot package. "These wrappings are silk." The archaeologist's eyes lit as the object came free.

It was a sword.

It was in remarkable shape. It gleamed as Nancy began wiping it down with her bandana. The blade was much the same as Rai's khukri dagger but twice the size. "It's a kopis," Nancy said. "One of the two major sword styles used by the Greeks." She looked over at the blade on Rai's belt. "Many scholars believe the khukri of Nepal is descended from it."

Rai scowled out of his bandages. "Greeks steal from us."

"Alexander was said to favor it," Nancy continued. "This one is …" Nancy gaped in shock. "Hold the light closer!"

Bolan shone his light on the glittering weapon. There was an inscription along the blade. "What does it say?"

"It's in ancient Greek. It says 'Beautiful Alexander.'" She turned the blade over. "Here it says 'Hephaestion.'"

Blair peered over her shoulder. "What's that? Greek for infection or something?"

Nancy gazed heavenward for strength. "Hephaestion was Alexander's number one general, commander of the Companion Cavalry and his closest friend since childhood. They were assumed to be lovers."

"Yeah…" Blair leaned back. "I fast-forwarded through that part of the movie."

Bolan stared at the ancient weapon. "You have your provenance, Eckhart. The Russians may have gotten here first but they didn't know what they'd found."

Eckhart took the sword from Nancy's hand and brought it over for Penn and Beakman to look at. Bolan went to the antechamber while the academics oohed and aahed over the sword. It appeared to be a bathroom. A square bathtub big enough for two had been cut out of the rock and lined with tile. Bolan felt a pang of sympathy for the poor bastards whose job it had been to haul buckets of hot water up the spiral stairs. The most interesting thing about the room was that the tub was filled with rubble, and a five-foot section of the rock wall behind had been replaced by more concrete. By Bolan's estimate the back wall led straight into the heart of the mountain. He reached into the tub and picked up a fallen and slightly rusted tin placard. The trefoiled shape of the International Biohazard Symbol was emblazoned on the sign in scarlet.

The Executioner walked back into the master chamber and clicked his radio. "Piet, this is Cooper. What's your status?" There was no response and Bolan tried again. "Piet, this is Coop. Come back."

Team Endeavor heaved a collective relief as the radio crackled and the South African responded. "Cooper, this Piet. What is your status?"

"We are inside the Citadel. Looks like Eckhart was right all the way, but there are some things you need to see. What is your status?"

"Cooper, I need you to take a moment and consider your position very carefully."

Bolan's blood went cold but he kept it out of his voice. "What does that mean, Piet?"

"It means my employers have authorized me to negotiate the terms of your surrender."

14

Bolan shouted orders. "Blair! Get downstairs and tell everyone we have company coming! Send one of the cowboys up with the Dragunov and as many grenades and spare magazines as he can carry! I need the pick and the digging bar! Tell ZJ I need a breaching charge ASAP, two or three would be better if he has time! You're in command down there!"

Roy Blair might have been a jerk but he was an ex-Ranger and he'd experienced tunnel fighting in Afghanistan. He shot Bolan the toothpaste-selling grin. "Let's kick this pig."

Bolan nodded at Rai. "Go with him. I need every rifleman we've got down there."

The Gurkha looked to Eckhart and then nodded. Rai and Blair charged back down the passage.

"Coop." Bolan turned. Nancy was shaking. "What's going to happen?"

There was no point in lying. "The Chinese are going to assault. We have to survive it, give them a bloody nose and then maybe we can negotiate with them for real." Bolan gave her a smile. She had unconsciously drawn her pistol. In the other hand she held the glittering sword that had belonged to Alexander the Great.

"Listen. Your job is to guard that relic with your life. Team Endeavor found it. We're keeping it."

"You got it," she said firmly.

Two cowboys tottered into the chamber laden with weapons and tools. Bolan took the pick and tossed Yuli the pry-bar. The two men put their muscle against the sealed natural window in the rock. ZJ ran in with his canvas duffel bag. "Blair said you need charges?" he gasped.

The Executioner wiped his brow. "Yeah, I need one to unseal the wall in the bathroom. Take a look at it and make me another in case we meet another obstacle behind it."

ZJ disappeared into the antechamber. Yuli heaved and a huge chunk of concrete fell to the floor with a crash. The Russians had worked in haste and the rest came easily.

"Okay, we're in blackout up here from now on. Yuli, go down and help defend the main cavern, we'll give them hell from up here."

"*Da.*" Yuli took up his weapon.

Blair's voice came across the tactical. "I have movement in both forks of the ravine. They're putting the cave mouth in a crossfire."

Bolan breathed in the fresh air coming through

the unsealed crack in the rock and peered down. Men were indeed moving in the ravines. "Confirmed, we have a line of fire on them."

ZJ came back and gave Bolan a pair of packages the size of butter cubes. "Done. Charges are shaped. Strip the adhesive and pull the pin. You have a five-second fuse. The one in the antechamber is set and ready."

"Nice." Bolan kept his eyes on the enemy. "How are we downstairs?"

"Charges are set below. They aren't claymores but they will stop the first rush. I guarantee."

"Good, get on them." Bolan clicked his radio. "Blair."

"Yeah, boss?"

"I'm sending ZJ back down. Give the Chinese a bit of a firefight but not enough to stop them. When they get close ZJ hits them with the charges."

"Copy that."

Bolan checked the loads in his Dragunov and shouldered it as men began moving below. "Here they come! Give them a few bursts and fall back!" he radioed.

Grenade launchers thumped from the ravines and looped into the mouth of the cavern but Bolan trusted the team had taken cover using the stalagmites and rock formations under Blair's directions. Gunfire stuttered back but not enough to stop the assault. The Chinese came from both ravines and linked up in a wave firing as they came. Bolan could dimly hear Blair shouting down below.

"Fall back! Fall back! Fall back!"

It worked like a charm. The Chinese wave came on. ZJ fired his charges. The world flashed orange and Bolan leaned back as heat washed up the side of the mountain. The Chinese attack was over save for a few burned and blasted stragglers who tried to stagger back. Beakman and Eckhart leaned into the slit to take them. "Wait," Bolan whispered. Shots cracked out from the cavern mouth methodically. Three of the wounded fell. One managed to totter out of the line of fire and crawl behind some rocks. Bolan clicked his radio. "Blair, SITREP."

"They fell for it. I count eleven down. No wounded on our side."

"Copy that, hold position," Bolan ordered. Piet would have informed the Chinese of Team Endeavor's battered state and right now he would be telling them that most likely that was the last of the high-explosive. They would come again, and this time it would most likely go hand-to-hand in the caves.

He turned to Beakman and Eckhart. "We're surprise number two. They don't know about our firing loop up here, and once they do we're going to take counterfire from whatever heavy stuff they have. This time when they attack we go for the support weapons. Grenade launchers, machine guns, RPGs. When they fire we take them out. Got it?"

Both men nodded nervously.

"Nancy, take Penn and go into the bath. It's probably the safest place."

Penn sighed. He leaned awkwardly over the pile of ordnance on the floor and picked up a spare pistol. "I think I would prefer to stay out here and hand out water and ammo rather than be found hiding in the bathroom."

Nancy's jaw set. "Me, too."

"Okay, you're hired," Bolan said.

Blair's voice crackled across the radio. "Movement in the ravines, Coop. They're up to something."

"Copy that." The ravines faced the entrance to the Citadel like the forked tongue of a snake and they suddenly lit up to become tongues of fire. The eastern fork strobed with concentrated machine gun and automatic rifle fire. The west fork ignited with the signature fore and back blast of a recoilless rifle and its high explosive round shot straight into the Citadel. The stones vibrated under Bolan's boots. For a split second the rifle operators were alit with the blast from their weapon.

Bolan put his crosshairs on a gunner and squeezed the trigger. The Dragunov cracked and the weapon operator fell across his smoking tube. Gloom instantly descended again but Bolan took a wing shot on the loader. "Beakman! Hit 'em!"

Beakman shoved his weapon out the window slit and fired his grenade launcher. He lurched back as a hail of bullets whined and cracked against the stone. "Shit!"

"Blair!" Bolan shouted. "SITREP!"

"Yagi's down! One of the horse wranglers is dead! We—" Blair paused and shouted. "ZJ! Where's Rai?"

Bolan heard the Hungarian shout back over the line. "He's gone!"

A grenade launcher thumped below and spiraled its munition into the Citadel. Bolan caught the pale yellow flash and made the grenadier pay with his life as the Dragunov recoiled against his shoulder. He scanned for more targets. The west fork lit up again as the recoilless fired. He'd missed the loader.

"Shit!" Beakman shouted.

"Down!" Bolan roared. Beakman, Penn and Eckhart leaped for the stone furniture.

Nancy screamed as Bolan tackled her over one of the carved stone chairs. The 82 mm recoilless rifle round filled the chamber with light, heat and flying rock. Bolan's vision swam and his ears rang but he forced himself to his feet. Eckhart lay gasping on the floor but appeared unscathed. Beakman's head was bleeding a river but he hauled himself to his feet. He promptly sagged against a chair and dropped his rifle as he went into a coughing jag. Penn's ankle had left him a step too slow and most of the archaeologist was splattered across the chair and table he'd failed to take cover behind. The chevron shape of the window had been blown out into a four-foot diameter smoking hole.

Bolan scooped up his Dragunov. The optic glass of the scope was shattered and he tossed the weapon aside and replaced it with Beakman's rifle/grenade combo. He checked the load and stepped to the hole. The west fork rippled with orange fire and another recoilless round hit the cavern mouth below like a thunderbolt.

The Executioner fired. For a split second he could see the tiny figures of the loader and his new assistant looked up at the little puff of flame on the mountainside. It was the last thing they saw as the frag shredded them.

Bolan stepped back as bullets smacked into the rock around him. "Blair!"

"We've fallen back!" he responded. "Yagi's all messed up!"

"Copy that! Eckhart's down and Beakman is marginal. The Chinese are going to charge us any second! I'll take as many as I can from here! If they get to the cave mouth hit it with white phosphorus!"

"Copy that!"

"Beakman!" Bolan shouted. "Can you shoot?"

Beakman leaned on the stone chair mechanically wiping blood from his eyes but curtains of it instantly ran down his split brow to replace it. He blinked at Bolan dazedly. He picked up Eckhart's rifle and focused. "Fuck these assholes." He picked up a canteen and poured half of it over his face.

In the ravines below the Chinese attack whistles blew. Bolan counted over two-dozen weapons below lighting up. He watched as the tracers streaked straight up into the sky. Paratroopers were descending out of the sky and the automatic weapons of the Chinese were ripping upward to meet them. Beakman blinked. "Tell me that's the 82nd Airborne."

"No." Bolan shook his head. "It's the Russians."

The Russians were being shredded out of their shrouds. Over half of the paratroopers were limp and drifting off-course and more were dying every second. The Chinese obviously had night-vision gear.

Bolan shouted orders into his radio. "Blair! Move everyone forward to the cave mouth! Yuli! Anyone who gets to the ground, call them in! Covering fire!" Bolan began looping grenades into the ravines to suppress the Chinese shooters. All cohesion in the Russian drop had been lost. Torn parachutes collapsed and men fell screaming to their doom while others who were dead or wounded smacked into the cliff sides with bone-breaking force and tumbled downward wrapped in their lines and canopies like death shrouds.

Still, some of the Russians were hitting the ground boots first and desperately trying to stay alive. The Chinese had too many targets and made the mistake of engaging all of them. They should have concentrated their fire on taking cavern and then taking the Russians at their leisure. Bolan and Beakman fired at every Chinese muzzle flash in the ravines but the Russians still died in droves.

Yuli's voice boomed through the canyon in Russian, calling the airborne to him. Out of what must have been a fifty-man airborne platoon fourteen ran for the cave mouth. Only five made it. Blair was instantly on the radio. Bolan could hear shouting in the background. "Coop, we need you down here. Now—"

Bolan handed the grenade launcher to Beakman. "Drop a frag on anything that moves outside."

Beakman took the smoking weapon. "Right."

Bolan went back down into the main cavern complex. Everyone was pointing guns at each other and the ranking Russian paratrooper was shouting at Yuli in a stone cold rage. Bolan left his rifle slung and walked up to the shouting man. "You're the ranking soldier?"

The Russian was short and powerfully built. His shaved head had a remarkable number of scars on it. He stood tall but did not salute. "I am Sergeant Vyachslav."

Bolan stared at him noncommittally. "What can I do you for, Sergeant?"

The Russian glared. "This is Russian facility!"

Bolan's eyes went cold as the grave. "This cave is mine. Your facility is upstairs." He glanced toward the mouth of the cavern. "You can go around."

The Russian simmered.

Bolan shrugged. "My cave and your facility are both in the sovereign republic of Tajikistan, and neither of us want them to be involved, do we, Sergeant?"

The Russian visibly calmed himself. He took a moment and peered around.

"So, tell me, Sergeant," Bolan asked.

"Tell what?"

"Where's your nuke?"

Vyachslav sputtered.

Bolan cut off any protestations. "First you vacuum-bombed us. Then you sent in a deep inter-diction chopper. Now that we found your facility, you drop in airborne." Bolan gave the sergeant a pointed look. "You guys are a suicide squad. You're here to end this. You're the final option. Where's the nuke?"

"Lost in drop." Vyachslav spoke through clenched teeth. "Presumed to be in enemy hands."

Bolan shook his head in disgust. "So what good are you?"

Vyachslav's body locked up.

Bolan eyed the Russian coldly. He understood the man's mission and in his heart he had sympathy for the soldier. But in the bowels of this cave he had no room for empathy in his negotiations and he shoved the point home. "You and your men want to stay here? You're going to have to earn your keep."

Vyachslav shook with rage. "My men and I are prepared to fight to the death."

"No." Bolan shook his head. "You and I are going upstairs. You're going to lead me through the facility. We're going to see if your bug is still viable."

"And if viable?" Vyachslav sneered in open sus-picion. "You take?"

"No."

The sergeant was taken aback. "No?"

"No. If your bug is still kicking—" Bolan let out a long breath as a very bad plan began forming in his head "—I'll go get you your nuke for you."

Vyachslav spent long moments trying to read the American warrior before him. There seemed to be no deception in his burning gaze, and it was a well-established belief in the Russian Special Forces community that God himself contended in vain with a man who was truly brave or truly insane.

Vyachslav was fairly certain the man before him was both.

"That would be good trick," the Russian admitted.

15

Bolan blew the charge in Alexander the Great's bathroom. ZJ had done well and the cement seal blew inward in a five-foot lozenge of shattered concrete. Bolan shined the tactical light on his rifle into the clouds of dust. Behind the cement was far more rubble than the small charge had brought down. Much of it was cement as well as rock. Filing cabinets, tables and chairs, and broken equipment lay amongst the rubble as well. The Russians had unknowingly built their facility above the cavern complex. It looked as if an earthquake had collapsed one of the caverns and taken a facility floor with it. The Russians seemed to have discovered the Dark Citadel of Alexander the Great and lost control of the Fourth Horseman of the Apocalypse right about the same time.

They had also conveniently left a ladder up into the collapsed room above and had obviously intended to come back in the future.

"I go first!" Vyachslav snarled.

Bolan rolled his eyes up towards the shattered plague city above. "By all means."

The sergeant gave Bolan a sour look as he pushed past.

"You have a map of the facility, Sergeant?" Bolan asked.

"*Da,*" the paratrooper growled.

"Can I see it?"

"*Nyet!*"

Bolan sighed wearily at the belligerent Russian. "Yo, Ivan." Vyachslav turned to see Bolan's AK pointed between his eyes. The Executioner pushed the selector to full auto for emphasis. "Go play with the Chinese."

The Russian appeared to consider his own slung weapon but thought better of it.

Bolan spoke quietly. "We both want the same thing. We have to do this together or not at all. If we don't, the old men in Beijing win and both our nations lose." Bolan lowered his weapon and held out his hand. "The virus must be destroyed or delivered back to the control of your government. Whichever is more expedient. Agreed?"

The Russian spent long moments sizing up Bolan again. He finally shoved out his hand and shook. "*Da,* agreed."

"If your people were expecting to come back and take care of this properly, I'm thinking the generators haven't been disabled."

"I believe this is correct," the Russian said.

"Then let's turn on the lights." Bolan held the ladder while the Russian climbed and then followed him. He climbed past eroding, sandy cement and pencil-thin rusted rebar that spoke of Soviet-era cost cutting. Cost cutting on their nuclear, chemical and biological facilities had cost the former USSR far more than it had ever saved, and it was still costing them to this day. This night it had cost them dearly in a mountain pass that most of the world had never heard of.

Vyachslav held out his hand and pulled Bolan up into the ruins of what looked like a file room.

Most of the doors were open.

Bolan suspected that once the outbreak had occurred the place had gone into lockdown, but once the infected were sealed inside they had wandered about during their last days. The two men moved through the facility. In the kitchen they found the dried remnants of food still on the stovetop. They found an exercise area, a communications room and a tiny armory. Most of the interior windows were shattered and glass crunched beneath their boots from broken overhead lighting. Most of the walls and floors showed cracking and earthquake damage. They found the bodies in the dormitory. The air-cured and mummified bodies lay in their deathbeds. The horrible pitting in their desiccated skin gave evidence to the terrible way they had died. The two soldiers moved on to the generator room and Vyachslav checked the gauges on the green box the size of a bank vault. "Fuel bunker almost depleted. Evaporation has occurred."

Bolan shook his head. "We won't be staying long."

"Da." The Russian pushed the power button and current snapped within the generator. The engine began to cough, vibrate and whine into life. The surviving fluorescent lighting clicked on block by block and threw the facility into alternating harsh glare and shadow.

They finally came to the lab. It wasn't particularly impressive. Unlike a chemical or nuclear facility there was very little to see save a room full of what looked like medical equipment. The main point of interest was the thick wall that split the room in half. The wall had a thick steel door and a massive panoramic window of equally thick glass. Both rooms were painted the same calm inducing blue they had slapped on everything from cockpit panels to insane asylums.

Bolan picked up a thick binder from a worktable and peered at it. Vyachslav rose up on his toes to try and peer over Bolan's shoulder. "What does file say?"

"Dunno." Bolan shrugged and held out the binder. "It's in Russian."

Vyachslav took the binder and his brows bunched mightily as he flipped from page to page and struggled to translate. "It is very technical. Table on this page say fifty percent increase in infection rate predicted."

The only good thing to say about smallpox was that unlike the common cold or flu viruses it wasn't that easy to contract. It generally required direct or prolonged contact with someone or clothing and bedding used by someone who was infected. The first stage to making a weapon out of it was to get it airborne and easy to contract. It appeared the Russians had made headway. "Look for anything on viability, replication or life cycle," Bolan said.

"Ah." The Russian flipped to a green tab and scowled at the dense Cyrillic text. "I am not sure, but I believe implication is virus can..." He struggled for English words. "Go to sleep."

Bolan nodded. "Go dormant."

"Yes...dormant...in suitable moist environment until reactivation and introduction to human host."

Bolan pointed across the lab to the hot zone. Behind the massively thick glass were centrifuges, all sorts of scientific equipment and a glass dome containing what looked like a rack of twelve, sealed test tubes. "I think that's our suitable dormancy environment."

Vyachslav bunched his brows at the tubes of blue goo. *"Da."*

"For the sake of argument I'm going to say thirty years of dry air and no host has killed any virus in the caverns or the facility." Bolan nodded at the hot zone. "I'm saying the stuff in there is viable."

"Da." The Russian folded his arms and glared at the goo. "How do you suppose outbreak occurred?"

"I don't know. The earthquake was strong enough

to drop an entire room. Maybe someone in here dropped something. Maybe they panicked and ran rather than follow containment protocol. Then everyone had it."

The sergeant pulled out a white plastic card key tethered around his neck. "Can we destroy?"

Bolan had been giving that some thought. They were out of white phosphorus and there was very little in the lab to fuel a fire. Taking all the viral samples down to the kitchen and boiling them was somewhat problematic and even then the Chinese could still probably retrieve data from the computers and the safes that Bolan was unwilling to let them have. Bolan let out a weary sigh. "Looks like I'm going to have to go get that nuke for you."

THE EXECUTIONER CAME OUT under a white flag of truce. Piet Van stood alone a few dozen yards away from the entrance. A red flare guttered and sparked in the dirt at his feet. His left arm was still in a sling and he held a cigarette in his right hand. Bolan's Stetchkin machine pistol was thrust under his belt cocked and set on full auto. "Coop. Good to see you alive," the South African said.

Bolan hadn't come to exchange pleasantries. Nor was he going to go into recriminations or hurt feelings. Piet had been a mercenary for decades. The three things that concerned him most were money, life and death. Bolan was prepared to speak to the man in his own language.

"You know what's in there?" he asked.

"What's in there?" Piet smiled sadly and shrugged his good shoulder. "Alexander the Great's brass-plated piss-pot? King Solomon's mines? My mother's long lost virginity? Who cares, man? Job's a job. I like you, Coop, and it grieves me that two reasonable men such as ourselves are on opposite sides of this. Eckhart may be a billionaire and I suspect you're well-connected, but what's left of Team Endeavor? You're out here on your ace, man. So I'll tell you. Surrender, you and all your lot in there. I give my word there will be no reprisals."

Despite the man's betrayal Bolan was tempted to believe the South African was negotiating sincerely. On the other hand Bolan had grave doubts about the intentions of the men in Beijing giving orders, and this was definitely a "no witnesses left alive" situation.

He glanced around at the blasted bodies still littering the ground at the cave entrance. "I think we took out about a squad. Count the guys we killed in the ravines maybe two squads, and we just got reinforcements. You really think you can dig us out before the Kremlin finally goes ape-fire and sends in the entire 76th Air Assault Division?"

"Well, Coop? Just between me, you and the lamppost? That scumbag opium lord? Shukrat? Well he and the Chinese did a deal. They crossed his palm with gold and promised him more. He came in this morning with his personal army. Thirty men, and they're dripping in RPGs. If you want to surrender you had better do it now."

Bolan glanced into the mountains behind Piet. "Tell me something."

"What's that?"

"Anybody watching us?"

"Oh, there's a guy named Song drawing a bead on you right now." Piet took a meditative drag on his smoke. "I've never seen him snipe, mind you, but he seems keen enough, and his kit is first-rate."

"Tell you what. Put yourself between me and him."

Piet laughed. "Not bloody likely."

Bolan's voice dropped low. "I want to show you something."

Something in Bolan's burning blue gaze got through to Piet. He threw his cigarette to the ground and took two steps to his right to crush it beneath his boot before turning to face Bolan. His good hand went to the Stetchkin. "Oh, this had better be magic."

"Oh, it's magic." Bolan began unbuttoning his shirt.

Piet snorted. "You have a big, red *S* painted under there?"

What he had under his shirt was the biohazard warning placard from Alexander the Great's bathroom. Bolan watched coldly as the South African's pale eyes went wide. "You know what that is, don't you."

Piet stared fixedly at the international danger symbol. "That was in there, then?"

"It's smallpox in there, then. And it's been weaponized. The Russians had a secret facility above the Citadel. They dug into the mountain from the top down. There was an earthquake. They had an outbreak and discovered the Citadel below at about the same time. They sealed the place but then lost control of the facility with Tajikistan's independence before they could come back and clean it up. There are only two known sources of viable smallpox on this planet, Piet. One is in at the Center for Disease Control in the United States. The other is believed to be in Russia at a facility above the Arctic Circle. Your Chinese employers found about this place and decided they want to join the lethal bug club."

"Smallpox." The South African's shoulders sagged wearily. Africa was the last continent to have eradicated the virus. He'd likely seen people die of it in his lifetime. "You sure of this?" he asked.

"I can show you the blistered bodies."

"Well...*kak.*" Piet took a few moments to fish out a fresh cigarette and light it. He shook his head again and blew smoke. "You sure know how to knock up a party, Yank."

"So what are you going to do?" Bolan asked.

"Well, just what do you expect me to do, then?" Piet snarled.

"I've got a Russian Special Forces sergeant who says he lost his nuke during the drop." Bolan smiled coldly in the face of the South African's anger. "I want it."

"Oh, you expect me to hand-deliver it, then."

"No, I'll come get it."

Piet rolled his eyes. "That would be a good trick."

Bolan sighed inwardly. It was the current consensus of opinion. "It would be easier if you lend a hand."

"Why should I?"

"Piet, that's smallpox in there. The Chinese want it. And when they get it they're not going to want any mercenaries running around telling tales in bars. You're dead and you know it. Your only chance is with us."

Piet sneered skeptically. "Oh, and you're just going to let bygones be bygones, then?"

Bolan nodded sadly. "You know? It grieves me that two reasonable men such as ourselves are on opposite sides of this."

"So what do you expect me to do about it, then, Coop?" Piet asked.

"I'm going back. Tell your people I'm going to try to convince my team to surrender. Tell them you know me, and even if my group refuses you're pretty sure I can be convinced to betray them given a good enough deal. That should buy us a little time. Put your tactical on vibrate and keep it close. You'll know when I'm coming."

"Oh, and when you come? Then what?"

Bolan regarded the South African honestly. "I'm really hoping you'll think of something."

16

The Executioner climbed through the darkness. The rusted iron rungs set in the cement face rose a hundred feet toward the crest. The Russian facility had been bored into the mountain from the top down using the same building techniques used in constructing underground missile silos. It could only be resupplied by helicopter from the outside. All he was carrying was rope, a sound-suppressed Makarov and a bayonet. When he reached the top of the shaft he was confronted by clamshell doors. A catwalk encircled the top and a control panel set in the wall had big red and green buttons for controlling the doors but Bolan could see the seam of slag where the doors had been welded shut. It had been a rush job and the weld on both ends of the door only went out as far as the welder could reach. The Executioner's main concern was that the Russians might also have hastily poured a ton or two of cement on top.

He cut his last cake of explosive in two and

molded it into thin ropes that he pressed against the weld on both sides. The key was to shatter the weld without throwing the doors out of alignment and jamming them. He clicked in his detonator pins and pushed the button. Rather than the hissing crack of flexible charge Bolan got a deafening pair of double booms that rang the doors like a bell and echoed up and down the shaft like thunder.

Bolan blinked and spat against the cloud of roiling dust and played his light on the cargo doors. The edges were twisted and blackened but seemed free of weld. He pushed the green button. The clamshell cargo doors moaned and shuddered as chains and gears that had not seen maintenance in thirty years snapped off rust and ground against each other without the benefit of lubrication. The doors drew back to reveal the purple light of dawn. The crest of the mountain was a crown of jagged spires. The platform above was too small to land a helicopter but a crane rusted burnt orange with disuse was cleverly folded beneath an outcropping and there was plenty of room to lower large cargo from a heavy lift helicopter.

Bolan mounted a recessed ladder and gazed over the mountains. For a trained man, the climb up the shaft and the descent down the mountain would be more drudgery than technical climbing. For a sedentary scientist just the ladder climb would be exhausting, and when he reached the crest all he would see would be the endless, empty mountains and valleys of the Pamir range and realize his life was utterly dependent on the supply lifts sent by Moscow.

Bolan chose a path out of view of the ravines and began his descent. It wasn't hard and he had rope but he was racing the sun. He was losing and he still had to make his approach on the Chinese positions in the ravines. He moved from chute to seam, outcrop to slope; roping off and rappelling when he ran out of hand and footholds.

The sky went from purple, to blue, to red and then orange before he hit the rock formations at the foot of the mountain and he steamed with sweat in the dawn chill. He had sighted his path from the vantage of Alexander's chamber and he threaded it now as quickly as he dared.

The sun had fully risen by the time he circled back beyond where the ravine forked.

Bolan clicked transmit on his radio once for Piet's benefit and crept along the rim of the southern ravine. The Chinese had a detachment in both trails. Each had made camps and he could see a few tents the same reds and oranges of the canyon walls they clung to. They had made use of every overhang and rock outcropping and it would take some very clever satellite imaging from an operator who knew what he was looking for to find them. A plane would never see them. Most of the Chinese and Tajik tribesman were dug in at the ravine mouths. Those that weren't were in the tents and lean-tos were servicing weapons and gear or taking a quick, cold meal. Piet Van was leaning against a rock formation in plain sight and smoking cigarettes like he hadn't a care in the world. Bolan noted the rocks he leaned against formed a chute up to the ravine rim. He made for the chute and then down the rain-slickened rock one silent step at a time.

The Executioner spoke very quietly. "Hey, Piet."

The ex-commando spoke without looking around. "Beginning to think you wouldn't make it."

"Where's the nuke?"

Piet's head tilted toward a yurtlike construction that was doing a remarkable job of looking like an immense boulder. "Right in that tent behind us," he whispered.

"How many guards?"

"Two Chinese, both of whom will likely take a dim view of you."

Bolan drew his bayonet and walked up to the back of the tent. He stabbed the tent at ankle height and ripped the bayonet up in a single slice of razor honed steel. He stepped through the slit with his Makarov drawn. Two men sat cross-legged on the tent floor drinking tea and pointing at diagrams in a manual. One was clearly Chinese while the other looked Tajik. Something that looked like a metal suitcase painted Russian dark military green and swathed in pack webbing lay on the tent floor between them. Both men had just enough time to blink at the blue-eyed apparition in alarm.

Bolan took the Tajik in the temple as he raised his

knife. The Chinese officer opened his mouth to shout while fumbling for his weapon and Bolan shot. The officer fell flailing and gagging and Bolan finished the job with a shot through the forehead. He put a full magazine into his pistol and emerged from the back of the tent with the nuke and a Chinese poncho.

Piet nodded in admiration. "So, you're just going to strap on that firecracker and run for the cave, then?"

"Yeah, that's pretty much the plan," the Executioner replied. It wasn't a particularly good one, but the demolition charge weighed a good seventy pounds plus and he would never be able to climb back up the rock face to the Russian facility with it. Bolan grunted as he shrugged the weapon onto his shoulders and pulled the poncho around it in a futile attempt to make it look like a pack. "Team Endeavor will be dropping smoke and giving us some covering fire from the caves," he said.

"Figured you might say that." The South African inclined his head back toward the Citadel as he tucked in the corners of the poncho. "Lot of dead ground to cross. We'll need an ace up our sleeve."

Bolan raised a hopeful eyebrow. "You got one?"

Piet smiled slyly. "Well, I checked the perimeter this morning, and as I did I just happened to turn a few of what the Chinese use for claymores the wrong way about. I have a detonator for them as well. That should occupy them for a few seconds."

Piet frowned. "It's that fellow Song, the sniper, we have to worry about. He went walkies about an hour before dawn. He's out there. He's lurking. We're lucky he didn't see you."

"Or else he did and he's waiting to see whether I'm betraying my people or you are," Bolan said.

Piet grimaced. "There is that."

The big American clicked Send on his tactical twice to let Team Endeavor know they were on their way. "Let's go see what happens," he said.

The two men walked through the camp. A trio of Shukrat's tribal soldiers looked up from beneath a lean-to as they passed. They had no idea who Bolan was but Piet was a known intelligence asset around the camp. Piet shook out a cigarette nonchalantly and lit up. Bolan nodded. "Gimme one of those." He had given up smoking a long time ago but if there was ever a time to go casual now was it.

They passed a Chinese soldier who was swabbing out the barrel of his grenade launcher. He gave the two Caucasians a very suspicious look. Bolan blew smoke and pointed at the blown-out hole in the mountain that had been Alexander's bedroom window. Piet nodded as if he were receiving tactical wisdom and they kept walking toward the mouth of the ravine. It was infested with Chinese shock troops and Shukrat's tribal warriors. A short, thin man with his field cap turned backwards became aware of Bolan and Piet's approach and scowled ferociously.

Bolan eyed the walls of the ravine. "Can you walk us out of the line of fire of the claymores?"

"I can try."

"Who's the guy giving us the stink-eye?"

"That's Captain Tien-Ho," Piet whispered. "He speaks English, Russian and Tajik. There's a reason they gave him this job. Don't underestimate him," Piet warned.

"I won't."

Captain Tien-Ho bounced to his feet and stalked forward. He pointed his pistol at Bolan. "What fuck, Piet! How did this man—"

The ravine erupted in alarm.

"Run!" Piet shouted.

Bolan didn't need to be told. He shot the captain as he broke into a sprint. Weapons were spinning about on Bolan and Piet from every direction as Piet shouted, "Down!"

Bolan hugged dirt as Piet pumped his detonator.

Chinese antipersonnel mines slammed in both ravines and thousands of steel ball bearings ripped through the ravines. Bolan felt several pluck at the top of his pack. He grabbed Piet by his belt and yanked the South African to his feet.

The two soldiers ran for their lives.

Blair was on the ball and smoke grenades were already blooming in the dead ground between the Citadel and the ravines. The claymores had caught the Chinese and Tajiks by surprise but many of them had been dug in. The only good news was that most of them didn't know what was going on. Bolan and Piet both shot several opponents and charged into the open ground.

The high-power rifle bullet hit Bolan directly between the shoulder blades.

Luckily he had a thermonuclear weapon between himself and the rifle round. Nuclear demolition rounds were meant to destroy dams and bunkers. Once their timers were set and the demo team had prudently fled the scene you didn't want the enemy walking up and turning them off so the Russians encased theirs in titanium.

Bolan staggered as the bullet slammed into his burden. The Chinese sniper had gone active. Song's second round hit a moment later and a few inches higher and sent Bolan sliding face first into the dirt. Piet yanked him back to his feet with his good arm. The two men charged forward on wooden legs, heading for the obscuring shelter of the purple and yellow marking smoke. Bullets whined and cracked all around them. Bullets ripped past them in covering fire from the cavern and the window in the mountain but it wasn't enough. They just weren't going to make it.

Suddenly a Predator unmanned aerial vehicle dropped out of the sky like a hawk.

A cylinder the size of a mini-beer keg dropped from beneath one wing but it thudded to the sand inertly and Bolan noted the carrying handle on its side. He noted with greater interest the 2.5 inch

Hydra rocket pod beneath the other wing. The Predator cruised yards above the ground and its camera lens peered straight at Bolan and the remotely manned plane waggled its wings in recognition. Six rockets rippled out of the pod into the western fork of the ravine and as the Predator passed overhead it jinked and fired its remaining six into the eastern end.

The Predator did a victory roll as it soared over the ravine.

Bolan red-lined into his load-bearing tolerance as he snatched the carrying handle on the cargo pod and he and Piet ran into the smoke. They choked, gagged and staggered through the surreal, Crayola-colored world of the marking smoke and made for the cavern mouth on autopilot.

The Executioner knew he was inside when he was pulled out of the line of fire and thrown to the cave floor. He blinked hot smoke particulate out of his eyes and suddenly a canteen was being emptied into his face. Bolan forced himself to keep his eyes open and his vision went from blind, to besmeared to just been pepper-sprayed, but he could see. The first thing he beheld was Blair. The ex-Ranger tossed away the empty canteen and grinned maniacally as held out his hand. "Coop? You are one bad motherfucker!"

"Thanks." Bolan let Blair haul him to his feet and he shucked off the nuke. The claymores, the loss of their commanding officer and the nuke would leave the Chinese in disarray for a few minutes. But soon they would be coming with everything they had.

"Blair, I have to go upstairs where I can get a signal and then try and arm this nuke. I need you to hold them. Hold them as long as you can." Bolan locked eyes with him. "Hold to the last man."

Blair paused for the barest of seconds. "Copy that." The ex-Ranger's usual arrogance was gone. "Gimme every rifle, grenade and spare mag you got."

The remaining weapons were quickly stockpiled. Vyachslav gave his four remaining men a quick speech about their duty to the Motherland and the Russians fixed their bayonets. Yagi, Blair and Yuli did the same. Bolan turned to his demo man. "ZJ? You're with me. Once we get the nuke armed we'll come back down and lend a hand."

The little Hungarian nodded grimly. "Yes."

Bolan turned to the civilians. "There's a chance I may be able to get a signal out, but rescue will still be hours away. You need to get up top. The nuke is small. It will incinerate the lab and collapse the caverns but it won't bring down the whole mountain. You need to get away from the main access shaft because the blast may vent. Got it?"

Eckhart nodded. "Got it."

Bolan turned to the last order of business. "Yuli? Tell the guide to send the horses out. Then he's going up and out up top with the civilians."

Yuli spoke to the young man. The boy shot Bolan a betrayed look. He might be barely sixteen and he looked like a strong wind would knock him over but he had proven his toughness on the trail and under fire. His fellow tribesman and family members were dead. Honor demanded he stay and fight. Bolan nodded at him. "Yuli, tell him I know he's brave, but he's the ranking guide now. Tell him the others won't survive in these mountains without him, and he has obligations to his charges."

The boy squared his shoulders as Yuli explained his duty to him and then went to what remained of Team Endeavor's herd. The horses had been cooped up in a cave for forty-eight hours. They need very little encouragement to head for daylight.

Sergeant Vyachslav set his rifle and magazines on the spares pile and checked the load in his pistol. He holstered it again and nodded at Bolan grimly. "I go into facility. I go with you." Sergeant Stepan Vyachslav knew his duty and obligations as well and it was clear to Bolan he had earned the Hero of the Russian Federation medal on his chest. The sergeant intended to sit on the nuke and make sure it went off. Bolan understood.

"Let's do this."

17

The Executioner and ZJ worked the nuke. There wasn't much time. The Russians had lost their two demo-qualified men in the jump but Bolan had retrieved the communications package the Predator had dropped. The lab had a radio for direct communication with Moscow. Yagi had connected its antenna to the communication package and the Farm's intelligence assets were at Bolan's disposal. They'd manned the Predator after noting satellite shots of the explosions in the valleys around the Citadel. The Chinese claymores allowed them to zero in on Bolan's location.

It had taken about ninety seconds to pull up the Russian demolition charge's make, model and operating instructions. ZJ had grown up under the communists and had taken enough Russian in school to understand them. The titanium casing of the nuke had two craters you could stick a golf ball into but the sniper rounds had failed to penetrate and everything appeared to be in working order.

ZJ fiddled with a row of dials. "This one dials the yield, from one kiloton to ten. How much do you want?"

The Stony Man team figured an explosion the equivalent of five thousand tons of TNT would do the job and do the least irradiating of the Pamir region. "Five," he said.

ZJ set the yield. "Timer?"

Blair's voice came across the tactical. Gunfire crackled in the background. "Be advised, Coop! Enemy is at the door!"

"Copy that, Blair." Bolan glanced at Kurtzman's image on the laptop from the communications package. "Bear, I have four civilians. How are we doing on an evac?"

"We had an AH-60 helicopter hot on the pad just in case you called. It is already inbound but you have an ETA of at least an hour."

Bolan glanced up at the huddle of Eckhart, Beakman, Nancy and the boy. Nancy was weeping. Eckhart and Beakman were clearly on the edge of staying to fight. "You heard the man. Eckhart, Beakman why are you still here? Take Nancy and the boy and get out."

"Time?" ZJ repeated.

Bolan considered the climb and the condition of the civilians. "Twenty minutes."

Vyachslav grunted. "Too long. Set timer for—"

ZJ shot the Russian twice in the chest. The sergeant collapsed to the floor. ZJ leaped three feet back and the smoking muzzle of the Makarov turned on the rest of the party.

Kurtzman couldn't see what was happening from his camera's view. "Striker! What's—"

The screen went black as ZJ put a bullet through it. He backed up another six feet. "Nancy, take everyone's pistol. One at a time. Drop them down the medical waste chute," he ordered.

Nancy glared at the Hungarian. "Fuck you."

ZJ shot Eckhart and the billionaire fell dead with a bullet through the brain. Nancy turned white. ZJ smiled. "Now be a good girl, Nancy." His eyes and his pistol stayed locked on Bolan. "Or he's next."

The Executioner calculated. ZJ was out of reach and had the drop on him. The Hungarian had five bullets left in his pistol and he knew what Bolan was thinking.

"You move? She's next," ZJ said.

Nancy gathered the pistols and dropped them down the chute.

Blair's voice crackled across the radio. "Coop! Yagi's gone! The Russians are gone! The Chinese are in the main cavern! Repeat! Chinese are in the main cavern! Yuli and I are making a fighting retreat chamber by chamber!"

ZJ waved his gun at Vyachslav. The Russian was gasping past sucking chest wounds. "Nancy, take the sergeant's card key. Go into the lab. Put some of the viral samples in a case or a box or whatever you can find. Do it carefully. Then bring them to me."

Nancy looked at Bolan. He nodded. "Do it."

"Coop! Blow this fucker!" Blair shouted across the tactical. "Coop! Come in!"

Bolan slowly shook his head. "ZJ, the Chinese will kill you."

"The Chinese will bargain when they see I have live virus in my hand." He tapped a bulge on his hip pocket. "Especially when they see I have a live grenade in the other. With this place blown up and the virus in their possession I don't think they will care too much about me or all the gold Piet said they were spreading around. Plus, once I'm on a horse?" The Hungarian shrugged immodestly. "They'll never catch me."

Nancy returned with an aluminum briefcase. "It holds six."

ZJ nodded. "Show me." She opened the case and six of the viral containers fit into slots cut in the pre-molded foam inside it.

"Close it." ZJ ordered. "Slide it to me."

Nancy shut the case and slid it across the lab floor.

Blair's voice was a hiss over the radio. "Cooper. Yuli's gone. I'm playing hide-and-seek with these fuckers but I'm running out of room and it won't take them long to find the way up. You going to light that candle or not?" Blair's voice dropped to a mutter and he clicked off.

"Lose the tacticals," ZJ ordered. Bolan and Beakman took off their radios and slid them across. Zoltan pointed his gun at Nancy. "You, one more thing."

Nancy spoke through clenched teeth. "What?"

"The sword. Give me the sword."

The archaeologist's knuckles went white.

Nancy took the sword from her pack and slid it across the floor to ZJ. The Hungarian took the wrapped blade and shoved it into his demo bag.

The Executioner had been waiting for any kind of opening but the Hungarian was Special Forces and offered none. Bolan was just going to have to dive into ZJ, take the bullets and hope Eckhart, Beakman and the boy could pile on and overpower him.

ZJ turned the dial on the charge to ten minutes and pushed it down. The nuclear demolition charge began the countdown. ZJ smiled and raised his pistol. "Nice knowing you," he said.

Beakman moved first.

The archaeologist charged the Hungarian and took a bullet for his trouble. Bolan's bayonet rang from its scabbard as he raced into motion. Beakman staggered and ZJ shoved the stricken archaeologist into Bolan's path. Bolan caught him with his left arm as he sagged. At the same time he threw his bayonet. The Russian steel clanged off the wall as the ZJ fled the lab.

Bolan took a vital second to look at Beakman's bleeding belly. "Tim! You're gut shot but you're not going to die. Put your hand on it, suck it up and go!

Nancy, you and the boy help him. You have to get up the shaft. You have to go now. I'll stop ZJ." Bolan scooped up his blade as he ran after the fleeing Hungarian. The man was nothing if not nimble but Bolan was larger and more powerful and he began to close in as he chased him through the facility.

ZJ suddenly spun at a corridor junction and took a shot. The big American slammed into the wall with bone-jarring force as he hurled himself to one side. He raised his bayonet for the throw but the Hungarian was already around the corner and heading for the caves below. Bolan resumed the chase.

By his count the Hungarian had two bullets left.

ZJ was sliding down the ladder as Bolan hit the collapsed file room. The Executioner took a wild chance and jumped to the rubble below. His boots slammed jarringly into rock and a bullet whined over his shoulder as he landed. Bolan rose for the throw but ZJ had already hurled himself through the breach into Alexander's bathroom. Bolan knew where the killing ground would be and raised his blade as he ran through the master chamber and lunged into the corridor.

ZJ spun at the top of the stairs and leveled his pistol. Bolan threw the bayonet. Knife throwing was a dicey proposition at the best of times and aerodynamics was just about the last thing the Russians had considered when designing their bayonets. He jerked to one side as ZJ fired but there was no room to dodge and Bolan felt a hot burn as something plucked at his chin. The bayonet clanked against the stone by ZJ's head and fell clattering down into the darkness of the staircase. Bolan brought the back of his hand to his chin and felt a sting as blood puddled onto his wrist. The little bullet had shaved him and shaved him close. It had come an inch from ripping off his jaw. He rose from his crouch and regarded the little Hungarian with an icy stare. "Give me the case," he said.

ZJ's pistol was racked open on an empty chamber and his bayonet was down in the caverns with his rifle and probably in the possession of the Chinese. Gunshots echoed below. It seemed Blair was still in the game. ZJ tossed his empty pistol aside and checked his watch. "I'm going to wait another sixty seconds for the Chinese to kill Blair. In the meantime…" He reached into his demo bag and the sword of Alexander the Great came out in his hand. "I'm going to cut your head off."

The Hungarian stalked forward, the ancient blade swung low and loose in his hand as gleaming and sharp as the day it had been put in storage.

Bolan turned and ran for the master bedroom. ZJ laughed. "What are you going to do? Jump out the window and fly?"

Bolan skidded into Alexander's chamber. He couldn't fly and even if he could climb down fast enough to evade ZJ's sword nothing was waiting at the bottom but irate Chinese soldiers and Shukrat's men.

The bodies were Bolan's objective. For want of a better place and out of respect Penn, Rai and Gilad lay shrouded in their sleeping bags on the stone bed. The team had stripped them of all useful gear and equipment. However, Rai's khukri dagger was a very personal piece of gear and Bolan had thought he should be buried with it. Bolan unzipped Rai's bag and took the blade from where it lay on his chest.

ZJ laughed as he came through the door. "Come now, Cooper, you must—" Steel clanged as their blades crossed. Bolan swung savagely again and again and drove the little Hungarian back with sledgehammer blows. ZJ had a foot of steel advantage and might have been army saber champion back in Hungary but the Greek Kopis in his hand curved the wrong way and Bolan had swung a khukri in battle before. The ancient sword rang in ZJ's hand as he desperately blocked Bolan's attack. The Hungarian was forced into the passageway and the narrow confines gave Bolan's smaller blade the advantage.

ZJ spat in Bolan's eyes. The Executioner forced himself to keep his eyes open and not turn his head or blink. The Hungarian snarled as Bolan's blade burned across his sword arm in answer and blood spattered the stone. The smaller man snapped a kick at Bolan's shin. Bolan saw it coming and accepted the pain as he slashed and ZJ hissed as he took a second cut to the same arm. Bolan limped forward looking for his next opening. ZJ was running out of room and running out of dirty tricks.

Blair's voice boomed in the passage. "What in the blue hell?"

ZJ flinched at the sound and Bolan sank his blade through the Hungarian's sternum. The man paled and the sword fell from his hand. The Executioner yanked and the khukri ripped free with a splintering of bone. ZJ crumpled and fell.

Blair was shocked. "Coop! You're supposed to be nuking this place, not having sword fights with goddamn Hungarians!"

Bolan wiped his blade off on ZJ's back. "He shot Eckhart, Beakman and Vyachslav, stole the virus and was going to sell it to the Chinese to save himself." He thrust his blade under his belt.

"Well then fuck the prick, I hated him anyway," Blair pronounced.

Bolan stripped ZJ of his grenade, scooped up everything and tossed it all into ZJ's bag. He checked his watch grimly. "We've got seven minutes before the nuke blows."

"Yeah and the Chinese are right behind me. They're armored up. Only head shots are stopping them," Blair said.

"We can't let them get to the nuke. If they do they might have enough time to bring it back down here and chuck it out the window. It would be enough to save the lab."

Blair unslung the giant shotgun from his back.

"Here, you take this thing. It weighs a ton." Bolan jacked out the buckshot and slid in four fresh rounds from the sling loops. Shouts in Chinese and Tajik echoed up the stairs. Blair looked around. "You want to make a stand here or upstairs?"

"Upstairs, there's more room to maneuver."

"Right." The two men ran for the lab. They climbed through the shattered bathroom wall and scaled the ladder up to the collapsed file room. Bullets ripped after them as they dived through the door. They pounded through the corridors and skidded into the lab. The timer on the suitcase nuke was ticking away. Bolan took out the case of six viral samples and set it next to the bomb then took out ZJ's white phosphorus grenade.

Vyachslav called out from the floor. "Give grenade to me." Blood spilled from his lips as he tried to speak through lungs filling with blood. "Put me on top of bomb. Put grenade beneath me. Then go."

Blair stared awestruck at the Russian.

Bolan looked the dying man in the eyes then nodded. "Do it."

The Russian groaned horribly as Blair rolled him over and dragged him on top of the nuclear demolition charge and the virus case. His head lolled as he coughed. He was close to passing out. Bolan pulled the pin on the grenade and pushed it cotter lever up beneath the Russian. "Sergeant."

Vyachslav's voice was a wet whisper. *"Da?"*

"What you did here will be made known to your people."

The dying soldier let out a gurgling breath. Whether Vyachslav had heard or not Bolan would never know. The Executioner rose and he and Blair ran for the shaft. They were down to five minutes. Shouts rang out in the facility behind them. Blair spun and fired a burst down the corridor. The Chinese soldier lurched but didn't fall as he took the hits in the chest. Blair tossed his spent weapon away. "I'm empty!"

"Go!" Bolan knelt with the giant shotgun. Two more soldiers came pounding around the corridor junction and the Chinese trio came on. The 23 mm shotgun sounded like a cannon as it went off. The blast shattered the man in front and sent him flying into his two comrades. Bolan pumped the action twice and the other two soldiers died as solid steel thunderbolts smashed them into ruins. Bolan heard the sudden pop, hiss and whoosh of a white-phosphorus grenade back in the lab and the sound of men screaming as they were burned alive. Bolan turned and ran for the shaft. Sunlight spilled down the vertical tunnel. He tossed away the shotgun and got to climbing.

They were down to four minutes.

The rungs were wet with Beakman's blood. Bolan grabbed iron and hauled himself aloft. Blair was flinging himself upward like an orangutan. Bolan grimaced as he climbed. The rest of Team

Endeavor was barely halfway up. Beakman was los-ing blood in a steady trickle and could barely move. Nancy Rhynman was an accomplished equestrian but a two-hundred-foot ladder-climb would have taxed her on the best of days and the young Tajik guide was doing most of the work for all three of them.

Blair overtook them in thirty seconds.

Beakman let out a gasp as the ex-Ranger seized him and threw him into a fireman's carry. Blair shouted, "Hold on, Beakman!" and resumed climb-ing as if he was carrying his lunch. Bolan caught up with Nancy. She was weeping with effort and the young guide was tugging her upward and shouting encouragement in his own language. Bolan put his left shoulder beneath the archaeologist's backside and began pushing her up.

"Climb! Climb! Climb!" he shouted at everyone.

Nancy struggled with exhaustion but Bolan was an implacable force beneath her and he was taking enough of her weight that she moved hand over hand and put her feet rung to rung. The rungs were slick and Bolan snarled with effort as he climbed. He was too busy to look at his watch but his mental clock was ticking off the time. They were down to about one minute and he and Nancy weren't going to beat the nuke. He simply concentrated on moving. Depending on how the facility collapsed every foot could mean the difference between life and death.

Blair suddenly dropped down next to Bolan like

Spider-Man. "Hey, boss!" He rammed his right shoulder beneath Nancy's rear end and shouted up at her. "Just use your hands!"

Bolan and Blair hauled Nancy upward side by side, shoulder to shoulder.

With thirty seconds left she toppled forward off their shoulders. Bolan and Blair vaulted to the platform and yanked her to her feet as she quaked with adrenaline and lactic acid reaction. Their guide was sagging beneath Beakman's bleeding weight and unsure what to do. To the left was where Bolan had climbed around to get behind the Chinese camp but there was no time to pack Nancy and Beakman up the rock face. To the right it was a steep but easy slope; but that was where the lab was closest and the Citadel opened into the ravines. Time was the ruling god of their lives. Bolan jerked his head at the easier rock slope. "Go! Go! Go!"

Between them Bolan, Blair and their guide heaved Nancy and Beakman up the smooth rock. Bolan pointed over the side at an outcropping of rocks. "There!" The team mostly fell down the twenty feet of mountainside and tumbled into the rocks. Beakman coughed up blood and Bolan put his hand on the archaeologist's stomach to apply more pressure.

Blair glanced around in confusion. "Shouldn't we be blown up by now?"

Nancy yelped as the mountain jolted beneath them. Everyone looked around.

Blair shrugged. "Well, that wasn't so bad, more like a hiccup than a—"

The mountain began vibrating. Sand sifted out of crevices and rocks and pebbles began rolling down the hill.

"Hug rock!" Bolan ordered.

What was left of Team Endeavor clung to the side of the mountain as its bowels were ripped out from the inside. Bolan squinted against dust and sand and waited for the end but they caught a break. The lab had collapsed in upon itself and prevented a volcano-like eruption up the shaft. That didn't mean the five-kiloton explosion was without a place to go. The Executioner looked down as the roaring sound mounted.

Alexander the Great's bedroom window erupted in incandescent yellow fire. The entire chamber blasted out as the force channeled down through the cavern complex and sought to escape. A second later the cavern mouth of the Citadel shot fire like a dragon. The rock tunnels of the Citadel channeled and compressed the explosion like a nuclear pressure hose. The very air shook around them and Bolan squinted against the searing heat. The Chinese soldiers outside the cavern were instantly incinerated and their comrades in the ravines died a second later as the nuclear plume forked like a dragon's tongue and filled the dry arroyos with atomic fire. It was as if an entire mountain had grown rocket engines and was trying to blast off out of its moorings and take flight.

The jets of fire suddenly tapered off and turned to billowing black smoke as the explosion expended itself. Team Endeavor found themselves alive and relatively unharmed. Beakman clutched himself weakly and shook his head. "Now there's something you don't see every day."

"Okay, so we survived the explosion." Blair warily eyed the black smoke billowing up into the sky. "But are my kids going to be mutants?"

Bolan suspected Blair's children might indeed turn out to be mutants but the nuclear demolition charge that had collapsed the lab would probably have little to do with it. "No," he said watching the smoke rising toward them. He turned his eyes to the clouds approaching from the south. "But we don't want to breathe that. We need to get ourselves onto the other side of the mountain. Nancy and the kid are spent and we need to do it without killing Beakman."

Blair grinned at the insurmountable task. "Could be worse. Could be raining."

Thunder rumbled from the approaching storm clouds in answer. Bolan slowly turned his head and stared at the big, dumb ex-Ranger wearily.

Blair blinked into the collective glare of Team Endeavor. "What?"

18

Blair whooped and waved his arms like a maniac as the Predator drone flew over waggling its wings and the Special Forces AH-60 helicopter descended out of the sky. Rain was falling in sheets. The survivors clung shivering to a cliff on the mountain. The move had just about killed Beakman and he had passed out. The Blackhawk lowered its basket and winched Beakman aboard. Nancy and the guide went up one at a time after and then Bolan and Blair both stepped in and stood holding the cable rather than strapping in. The crew chief locked his hand around Bolan's wrist and hauled him aboard. He ran his eyes across the weary survivors and shouted over his rotors. "I was told you were twelve to fourteen!"

Bolan nodded wearily. "We were."

"Right." The crew chief was part of the U.S. Special Forces "night-stalkers." He understood all too well that sometimes not everyone made it back. He handed Bolan a blanket and nodded back at Beakman, where a medic was crouched over him giving him plasma and compressing his wound with dressings. "We'll get your man stabilized and a full medical team is prepped and waiting back at the base!"

The Executioner took the blanket and eased himself down next to Nancy and wrapped both of them in it. The crew chief spoke into his radio to the pilot and the Blackhawk dipped its nose and began powering south toward Afghanistan. An airman produced a thermos of coffee and Team Endeavor passed it around.

Nancy leaned back into Bolan and began to shake. "You all right?" he asked.

She leaned into Bolan's arms. "No one's ever going to know, are they?"

"No," Bolan said as he shook his head. "The Chinese and the Russians won't want anyone to know they were battling over a biological weapon. The U.S. government will deny any involvement. The Tajik government doesn't know about any of this and if they did they wouldn't want to. The lab, the Citadel and the story of Team Endeavor are buried, and they stay buried."

Nancy wept. "It was all so useless. Phil's dead. Professor Penn's dead, the Citadel is gone. Everything's just…gone."

"We stopped a biological arms race," Bolan said consolingly. "That's something to be proud of."

She wiped her face and nodded against Bolan's shoulder. "I know."

Bolan gave her a squeeze. "There's still the way

station we found. You can come back in a year. That ought to be good enough for an article in *Archaeology Today,* maybe even *National Geographic.* You can name it Eckhart's Cave. He'd like that."

She began crying again. "I will."

Bolan reached into ZJ's demo bag and drew out the bloodstained sword of Alexander the Great. "Besides, there're worse souvenirs to hang over the mantel."

Nancy's eyes grew huge.

Bolan shrugged. "I figured you've earned it. Now, let's go home."

Don Pendleton
EXTINCTION CRISIS

A brilliant conspiracy to seize the world's energy could also destroy it...

A powerful, sophisticated cadre of conspirators has accessed nuclear power plants across the globe and are poised to control the world's energy and raise hell. As the clock ticks down to worldwide meltdowns, Stony Man unleashes everything they've got in a race against a new face of terror.

STONY MAN®

Available December wherever books are sold.